The Reluctant Mafia King

Copyright

Opening Quote

How dare you say that my behavior's unacceptable? So condescending, unnecessarily critical. I have the tendency of getting very physical. So watch your step 'cause if I do, you'll need a miracle. You drain me dry and make me wonder why I'm even here. This double vision I was seeing is finally clear. You want to stay, but you know very well I want you gone. Not fit to fuckin' tread the ground that I am walking on.

Harder to Breathe by Maroon 5

Chapter One

⚔ Ryan ⚔

I look up at the slightly drunk woman above me. Her shoulder-length dark hair is mussed, and her cocoa-colored eyes are half-lidded and filled with lust. She licks her plump red lips seductively, and my eyes automatically follow the motion of her tongue.

"Oh, yes!" she breathes out on a soft moan as she slides herself up and down my cock. Her tits, though not that big, bounce and watching them makes me arch and thrust hard into her as I grip her hips and slam her down on my dick over and over again.

"Fuck," I whisper. I throw my head back as she starts twisting her hips and doing something with my dick that makes me want to come immediately. I slap her ass as she rides me, and her pussy clenches. I moan.

"Oh, God… Ryan… Oh!" I watch as she starts rubbing her own tits. I bite my lip as I pull her down. I want those hard peaks in my mouth. I run my teeth along one as I twist and tug the other. "Yes!" She tugs my hair as she keeps slamming herself down on me. I feel her tighten, and I groan.

"Fuck, don't you dare come yet." I slap her ass again as I sit up, pushing her up with me. Without pulling out, I swing my legs off the bed and stand with her wrapped around me. Her eyes widen when her back hits the wall near my bed.

"Oh, yes. Yes!" Her nails scratch across my shoulders. I relish the sting as I hold her against the wall and pound her tight pussy. "Ryan, I'm… gonna…" I slam harder into her. "Oh!" She uses her legs for leverage and meets every deep, hard, fast thrust I give her. Her nails dig into me as she throws her head back. I feel her clench and tighten around my length again. I slap her ass hard. "Fuck!"

"I said don't come."

"Ryan! Oh… yes… Yes! Yes!" Her voice. I hate her voice. It's high-pitched and whiny. I don't like her hair. I don't like her body. She's pretty and looks slightly angelic with a little bit of a demonic side, but she's not who I usually go for. I go for women with long hair who know exactly what I want from them. I like my women with curves, not stick-thin like this one. I love the women I fuck to have bigger tits. Tits I can bury my face in.

Unfortunately for me, my options at the Paradise Club tonight were very, very limited. No one caught my attention. Though, I seemed to attract every girl in the damn club. The only reason I brought Miss Insatiable Sex Drive home with me tonight is because I need the release. I always need the release after a job.

"Mmm… Fuck!" I slam into her a few more times. She clenches hard around my dick. "Come. Now," I command. I pin her against the wall. She clenches around me, and her pussy starts pulsing erratically. It's like she's grabbing my cock and sucking it into her. I come hard.

She screams. "Ryan! Fuck!" Her nails dig into my back, and she bites my shoulder as she thrusts herself over me while she comes. Even through the condom, I can feel her dripping down my cock. I finish and quickly pull out, even though she's still clenching hard around me. She whimpers and bites her lip as I let her down.

I walk into the bathroom, leaving the door open to keep an eye on her. I take the condom off and wrap it in toilet paper. Being from a rich and influential family, I've learned I can never be too cautious. I know how certain women can be. All they see when they look at me are dollar signs, a big dick, and a nice body. The easiest way to trap a man like me is to get

5

pregnant. That's why my condoms never leave my possession while a woman is here. I won't even throw them in the garbage in my private bathroom until the conquest of the night is gone.

I watch her as she pants and catches her breath. I finish cleaning up and make my way back into my bedroom, stopping at my walk-in closet to grab a pair of underwear from my dresser. I put them on, keeping my condom in my hand.

She bites her lip and walks towards me, sashaying her hips in what I assume is supposed to be something sexy to turn me on again. She leans against the closet door and lightly runs her hand over her chest as she squeezes her legs together.

"You sure you don't want to go one more round?" She shoots me a soft smile and licks her lip as she watches me pull up my black boxer briefs. I don't give her the satisfaction of even a smile as I slide a pair of gray sweats over my hips. I don't look her up and down. I'm done with her. I got what I wanted.

"I think three times is enough for me tonight, honey. Time for you to go. I got a busy day." I've never been disrespectful to a woman, but I've also never let one stay for longer than I need her to.

My reputation precedes me. Most women know what I want, and they still fall into bed with me anyway. No doubt to be the one that makes me fall in love, but no fucking way that's ever happening. I see my brother, Nick, and his girl. I don't want what he calls love. Arguing and making up only to be miserable again and tell everyone it's all good. Fuck. That.

She pouts and lets her eyes wander over my body. Standing at almost six feet five and having a body chiseled to perfection isn't an easy task. I train every day and spend my fair share of time in the gym. But even I know that all of the work I put into myself makes me drool-worthy and irresistible to most women. Being a twenty-year-old college student and heir to one of the richest and most powerful and dangerous mafias in the world has given me a confidence that many men only dream of. I'll be the first to admit that I take complete advantage of all the world has to offer me. Including the women falling at my feet on a nightly basis.

"Are you sure? You seemed all tense earlier. I'm happy to…" Her eyes drop to my dick, and she licks her lips. A cocky smile crosses my lips. "I'm happy to help you with that."

I slowly walk to her, not taking my eyes off the tongue that keeps darting out to lick her lips. I lean down like I'm going in for a kiss. She closes her eyes. I run my fingertips slowly down her ribs. She shivers and inhales sharply as she closes her eyes. I give her ass a squeeze. She jerks into me.

I smirk as I lean down so my lips brush across hers. "I said…" I swat her ass. She squeals as her body hits my chest. "You need to go. I have an early class. Get dressed. I'll walk you out."

She bites her lip and huffs as she turns. She swipes her panties off the floor and angrily puts them on. She glares over her shoulder as she reaches for her bra. "Are you going to make me walk? I didn't drive here. Remember?"

I laugh. "I'm not that much of an asshole. I'll have someone drive you."

I walk into the bathroom and throw my toilet paper wrapped condom in the wastebasket as I wait for her to finish dressing. When she's finally ready, I guide her out of my room and down the hall of the massive mansion that we call our family home. As I walk past my brother's room, the door swings open. I nearly collide with the pretty blonde storming out of his room. I raise an eyebrow as he trails behind her in nothing but his underwear.

"Care to take her down for me?" Jason asks. "I don't think she likes me much anymore." He gives her a cocky wink. She glares at him.

I laugh. "You will be telling me what happened."

"Sure. Tomorrow." Jason winks again with a cocky smirk. "Don't wake mom and dad. You know how pissy they get. Especially at…" He looks at his watch. "Three in the morning."

I groan. "Fuck. I have class at eight." I quickly usher the girls down the stairs.

When we pass the living room, I see a shadow figure sitting in the dark on the hearth by the fireplace. A fireplace is absolutely mandatory in Manhattan, where we call home. Winter can be a bitch when it comes to the cold. That fireplace has saved us all from frostbite on numerous different occasions. Thank God it's summer, though, because the two women I'm trying to load into the cars aren't making it easy.

"Are all of you Crane men dickheads, or is it just you and your brother?" the blonde asks.

I laugh as I lean into the car. "Probably just us." I wink just as arrogantly as Jason had as I close the door on her and walk back into the house without so much as a glance over my shoulder.

Once inside, I head straight for the living room and plop down in a chair near my other brother. "Nick."

"Ryan." He offers nothing more than the soft and slightly haunting utterance of my name.

"Does this have to do with Bitch-lope?" I ask.

He sighs. "You know her name is Penelope. Your stupid nickname for her is pissing me off."

I shrug. "If she'd stop acting like a bitch, I wouldn't call her one." I glance at the stairs as Jason walks down. At least he had the decency to put a pair of gym shorts on. He walks into the room and sits across from me.

"What's the deal? Penelo-slut do something to piss you off again?" I can hear the smirk in his voice. I bite my lip to keep from laughing.

Nick stands. "I don't know what unfortunate thing I did in my past life to deserve the two of you as brothers, but I'll gladly apologize for it every fucking day if it means you two disappear. I hate you. Both of you."

I laugh. "Oh come on. You know we love you."

Jason grabs Nick's arm and pulls him back down. "Spill. You'll feel better. What happened?"

We all give each other shit, but when it comes to family, we're always here for each other. No matter what.

Next to each other, we make a handsome set of brothers. We're all tall and muscular. We all have dark hair and chiseled features. Women fall at our feet. We're also all very intimidating. Most people don't fuck with us because they know who we are, but also because we don't look like the type of guys who take shit from anyone.

Nick sighs as he sits and puts his head in his hands. "Sometimes, I question what the hell I'm doing with a woman like her. I'm a kid from the wrong side of the tracks who lost his parents to some suspicious as fuck circumstances. I'm not this rich trust fund kid from a powerful family. I'm really a poor kid from the hood."

I shake my head. He gets like this after every fight he has with her. I don't really take too well to people fucking with my family. "Nick, you know better."

8

"Dude, she's playing you. She's using you. You know it. I know it. Ryan knows it. We all know it."

Nick shakes his head. "You guys don't know her like I do. She's had it rough. Sometimes she gets overwhelmed and lashes out."

"That's your romantic side talking." I stand and pat him on the shoulder. "You'll come to your senses one day. I hope it isn't too late."

"Shut the fuck up, Ryan," Nick growls. "Just because you and Jason fuck any female that walks don't mean you know shit about what it's like to be in love."

I turn back to him. "You're right. I don't know shit about what it's like to be in love. Because I'm smart enough not to fucking do it. When you're a man in a position of power like the three of us are and have so much money we don't know what to do with all of it, people will take advantage. That's what she's doing. You better wake up, Nick. She's after your trust fund." I turn back to the stairs and start climbing them to my room.

"Asshole," Nick mutters under his breath.

"He's right, Nick," Jason says.

"Neither of you know anything about this. You don't know her."

"It's easier being on the outside looking in. There are signs. You don't see them." Jason starts following me up the stairs, and I slow down a little so he can catch up. We walk towards our rooms. He turns to me when we reach his door. "Do you think he'll see it before she completely ruins him?"

I sigh and look up at the ceiling. "I honestly don't know. But we'll be here to pick up the pieces." Jason nods as he steps into his room and closes the door. I walk to mine and close myself in. I collapse on my bed with a satisfied and exhausted groan.

Seconds later, I'm passed out dreaming of where I can lead the Crane Mafia when I take control. No more late-night missions that involve me killing the members of other smaller gangs running drug deals in my family's territory. It's not like I have a problem taking out the bad guys. I have a problem taking the drugs and redistributing them to my own guys to sell. My operation will be legit.

The largest legit mafia this world has ever seen.

Chapter Two

☒ Jason ☒

I lean against the door to Ryan's room and groan. I need to stop drinking. Waking up with a pounding head and nauseated stomach is getting old.

I take a deep breath to choke down the rising bile and raise my fist to knock on my brother's door. He opens it before I get the chance. I immediately decide I hate him. I don't understand how he can, drink the same amount as me, probably more, get the same amount of sleep as me, and wake up bright-eyed and fucking bushy-tailed.

I glare. "Don't you look like the picture of the perfect college student today."

Ryan has the balls to laugh, and I glare harder. "Not my fault you can't hold your liquor."

"Fuck… You…" I turn and head for the stairs, nearly throwing up on the way.

Ryan follows, laughing. My mother is an awesome cook, but the smell of bacon wafting through the house right now makes me want to puke.

When we turn the corner for the dining room, Nick is sitting at the table grinning from ear to ear. I inwardly groan when I see Penelope.

Ryan, being as in your face as he is, doesn't hold back. "You still haven't found anyone you'd rather torture more than my brother?"

Penelope shoots Ryan a death glare. "Why do you hate me?"

Ryan sits and gives her a mock sweet smile. I bite my lip to keep from laughing as I sit next to him. "Hate you? I don't hate you. I despise you because I know your game. You want Nick's inheritance. Not him. All you see is dollar signs, sweetheart."

"Ryan," Nick warns. Penelope looks like she's about to cry, but I don't miss the hatred she shoots both of us. Ryan shrugs as our parents walk into the room. Mom puts warm croissants on the table, and my mouth almost waters.

"Damn. Mom. It smells so good," I say as I eye them. My stomach, however, doesn't agree. I fight back a groan and grab a croissant anyway. I put some butter on it and throw some bacon on my plate.

"Jason. Watch your mouth," mom says sternly. They say Ethan Crane, our father and the leader of our family's mafia, is a man to fear. But those people have never met our mother. Jenny Crane is the one my brothers and I truly back down to.

I glance up at her and bite my lip. "Sorry, ma'am."

"Nice to see you guys aren't dicks to all women," Penelope mutters under her breath.

"Nope. Just the skanky little money hungry ones," I say loud enough for only Ryan, Nick, and Penelope to hear. Ryan nearly chokes on his apple juice. Nick shoots me another withering glare as Penelope pouts.

"You two support your brother," dad commands. I take a bite of the warm croissant to stay quiet.

"We do support him, dad. That's why we're warning him off the gold-digger," Ryan says as he stands. He looks down at me. "Let's go. We're gonna be late." I grab my other croissant, reluctantly leaving the bacon when my stomach threatens to stage a revolt, and follow. We walk out to Ryan's Ferrari and jump in.

"He isn't going to leave her until she ruins him," I say as I buckle myself in.

"We can only do so much, Jas. The rest he just needs to see on his own."

"He's an eighteen-year-old kid who gets sex whenever he wants by a hot girl. He's not going to see anything past her pussy as long as she's rubbing it in his face," I seethe.

"Again. A lesson he needs to learn himself." Ryan pulls out of our driveway and heads towards the school. The University of New York. We all attend. I'm majoring in business. Ryan and Nick are undeclared.

I glance at my big brother as he weaves in and out of traffic. "When are you going to admit to yourself that you should be going to the Institute of Culinary Education?"

He shrugs. "What's the point? It's not like I'll ever get to own my own restaurant or be a Michelin Star chef."

I sigh. "You know as well as I do that isn't true. Dad would never force you to take over."

"Jason, I've been bred to take over. Ever since I was born twenty years ago. This is my future. I've come to accept that."

"Why can't you do what you want to before that? It's not like you'll be taking over tomorrow."

Ryan is quiet for a few moments before he sighs. "It's why I haven't declared business like dad wants me to."

I watch him for a few moments as he drives. "What aren't you telling me?"

He glances at me. "I'm thinking about enrolling at ICE, okay? I was thinking I'd start the fall semester." He grips the steering wheel a little harder. "I don't know how it's going to work with all of these missions, though."

I nod as I chew my lip. He's right. We've been on far more missions lately than we ever have been. It's like other mafia factions are coming out of the deepest depths of hell to fuck with my family for the simple reason that they think it's fun. I can't believe, after so many years, we have all these smaller gangs and mafias challenging us. It's not like they don't know who it is they're fucking around with. My family is well-known. Even the police don't mess with us. Though, I don't know if that's completely out of fear or if my dad has paid off the right people. All I know is that the NYPD gives us a wide berth.

"I think you need to do something for yourself, Ry. Even if you don't ever do anything with it. You're the best cook I know, and you've wanted to go to ICE ever since we were kids."

"I know. Okay? I know. But cooking is never going to be more than a hobby. I've always known that."

"That doesn't mean you shouldn't do what you want to with your life now. Why not go to culinary school and travel like you've always wanted to without the stress of this fucking life?"

"It's easier for you, Jas. You're not the one taking over." He shrugs again as he focuses on the road. I hate that I can see the entire weight of the world on my brother's shoulders, and there's nothing I can do about it. "We've all always known that you don't want this life. We know you're just helping out until you start your business." He parks in the campus parking lot and looks at me. "You've got your entire life in front of you."

"So do you."

"I have a life of being a crime boss in front of me."

I sigh and look at him. "It doesn't have to be, Ry. Dad would give control to someone else if you didn't want it."

He shakes his head. "Do you really think dad wants to see his legacy given to someone not in the family?"

"You can't always please dad, Ry." I open the door and step out. I pause before I close the door behind me and glance back at him. "You need to do things that make you happy, or you're going to make a pretty piss poor mafia boss. You won't be able to turn it legit like you want to because you won't care about it. You won't care about anything." I close the door and walk to my class.

When I get there, I drop my backpack on the ground and sigh heavily. Between last night and my massive hangover today, I have no doubts I won't make it through the entire day.

There are advantages to being an eighteen-year-old from a rich and powerful family. One of them is being able to get into any club I want to, having the pick of any woman I want, and getting served copious amounts of alcohol if I want it. It helps that the club my brothers and I frequent is owned by my family. The rule is as long as we don't drive home drunk and we all leave together, we can drink if we choose to.

That's a good thing for me because drinking after a mission that involves shooting anyone, even if they *are* the worst human to ever walk the Earth, is the only way I manage to cope. That and fucking a willing woman until neither of us can stand.

13

"You look like you're deep in thought," a soft voice says next to me. I glance at her as she sits next to me. Pretty blonde, but I can't remember her name, even though she's sat next to me all semester.

"Uh… yeah. It's been a bad morning."

She smiles softly. "Kelly."

"Right." I focus back on my hands. "Sorry."

"It's okay. I won't pretend to not know your reputation, or that I'm not your type."

I chuckle. "It isn't that. Truth is I…" I take a deep breath before I lean back and look at her. "My life isn't all it's cracked up to be. Sometimes I feel like I'm two people. At night, I'm one person. During the day I'm some rich kid who has the resources to get whatever he wants and act however he wants." I shake my head as the professor walks in. "It's fucked up. I just want to start my own life. Lead it the way I want on my own terms." I look back at her while the professor sets up and everyone gets settled. "Too much to ask?"

She smiles softly and shakes her head as she bites her lip. My eyes are automatically drawn to them. I mentally slap myself. "No. Not too much to ask. But my question to you is what's stopping you?"

I laugh as I focus back on the front of the room. "It's not as easy as that. I have responsibilities to my family."

"You act like your family has the ultimate say. Like you have no say in it yourself."

I'm quiet. Didn't I just tell Ryan the same damn thing? Fuck. If I don't want to be part of the mafia, why am I allowing my father to drag me into missions? Why am I not putting my foot down and leading my life the way I want to?

"It's funny. You just gave me my own advice. Maybe I should start listening to myself."

She drops a hand on my arm and gives me a gentle squeeze before pulling away. "You sound like you're a smart man. Maybe you should."

I barely hear anything the professor says as Kelly's words ring throughout my head. Getting my earlier advice to my brother thrown right back to me hits me hard. She's right. I'm right? I shake my head slightly. I need to take my own advice. My family knows I want to start my own company. They all know I'm interested in developing property and making it into something that can be enjoyed for years, and by many. Whether that be a mall or a multi-million-dollar condo complex, I've never really cared. So why am I allowing myself to run missions when I should be concentrating on my studies?

I'm doing nothing but running myself into the ground. I barely sleep. Even if we don't have a mission, I barely sleep. I can't get the faces out of my head. They haunt me. Their family haunts me. No matter who they are, how bad they are, they have a family. Some woman out there is missing her son. Some guy out there is missing his kid. A wife. A brother. A sister.

Everyone has someone who's dealing with their loss. Who am I to play God and take them away from their loved ones? How would I feel if someone took Ryan or Nick from me? I'd be devastated if I lost my dad or mom. So how can I continue to play mafia at night and be a normal college kid during the day?

Same reason as Ryan, if I'm being honest with myself. I may not like it, but it's who I am. It's where I come from. I can't tell my father, the one who raised me and loved me and made me the man I am today, that I can't or won't help him out if he needs me. It's not fair to him.

It certainly isn't fair to Ryan or Nick. Asking them to do it all on their own is selfish. I may not want this life, but I can't walk away from it just like that.

No.

I need to leave it, but I need to leave it so it's fair to everyone. I'd never be able to live with myself otherwise.

Chapter Three

⚔ Nick ⚔

The AR-15 strapped to my chest feels just as cold as the heart inside it. The heart that I force myself to close off when I'm on missions. If I allow myself to feel, then I'll end up a tortured soul like Jason. Our youngest brother isn't like Ryan and I. It gets to him. Every single mission. Every single scream. Every single bullet. He does it because he loves his family, but he isn't like us. He doesn't forget and move on.

I follow Ryan down a dark hall and into an even darker room. Shocking. Considering how many windows are in the house, I'd have thought this room would have been just as bathed in moonlight as the rest of the place. Except that hallway.

"I can't see shit," Ryan whispers.

"I don't even know where the fuck we are," I whisper back.

"Basement."

"How? No stairs."

"We walked down an incline."

"Huh…" I hadn't noticed. Fuck. I need to pay more attention. Can't expect to be as good as my big brother if I can't even tell I'm walking down a fucking incline.

"There's a false wall in this room according to our intel. Should be to the right," Ryan says.

I can barely make out Ryan's back as he moves to our right. I know better than to follow. I need to watch his back. Make sure no one sneaks up on us while he's finding the false wall. I keep one eye on my brother, and the other on the hallway.

"Level one and two clear," Jason's deep voice comes over our earpieces. "Cobra one and Cobra three are on the way down. Don't fucking get trigger happy, asshole."

I chuckle. "It would serve you right for making Penelope cry the other day."

"More where that came from."

"Both of you fucking focus. The Bird isn't going to catch himself," Ryan growls.

"Listen to Cobra two," dad chuckles. Ethan Crane may love us and let us get away with a lot of banter and brotherly competition, but he's serious as hell about missions and this mafia. Our job is to get our target, the Bird. The time for fucking around comes after. Right now, our focus is our target and survival.

"Got it," Ryan says just as dad and Jason make their way into the room. They both guard the door as I make my way into the room to back up Ryan. The wall he was feeling around for gives way and opens into a secret chamber.

"Damn," dad says.

"What the fuck?" Jason whispers.

My eyes widen, and I'm speechless. "How... the... fuck did we not know about this?" Ryan grunts as he kneels down in front of the young, frail woman on the floor.

I look around the small room in shock. My eyes widen when I recognize the girl he's in front of. "Fuck... She's in my fucking history class."

Ryan looks up at me as Jason and our dad guard the door. "How long has she been missing?"

I drop next to her and feel for a pulse on her neck. I don't care that Ryan just did it. I need to feel it for myself. "She hasn't been there this whole week." Her pulse is weak. Dangerously fucking weak. I look up at Ryan. "What do we do?"

17

"Cobra two to Cobra five. Get down here. Everyone else. Look for the Bird. He's not here." Ryan looks at me. "Help me get her up."

"Yeah." I help Ryan to gently pull her up, and it's only then that I can see her scratches and bruises. Barely, but they're prominent. Even in the dark I can see how fucked up she is. "Fuck, Ryan. What happened to her?"

He shakes his head. "I don't know, bro."

"Where's the Bird?" I ask.

"I don't know that either."

Jason lets our guard into the room. He glances at us and then the girl before glancing at dad. "Sir?"

"Take her out. Get her to the hospital. Go," dad says. The guard lifts the girl in his arms and leaves. "All teams cover Cobra five. Look for the Bird."

I let out a long breath. "Have we ever lost anyone before?"

Ryan and Jason glance at each other before we all look at dad. I can just make out him pinching the bridge of his nose. "No. At least not in a long time, son. Come. We need to find him."

We all sigh and follow. We check the rest of the rooms in the basement before making our way upstairs to meet the rest of our teams. There's a flurry of activity in the house, but no target. No Bird.

"How the hell did we miss this son of a bitch?" Jason asks, shaking his head in bewilderment.

"I don't know, Jas. We've almost always gotten our guy. Since I've been on missions, we never failed. This is just as new for me as it is for you," Ryan says.

"Everyone clear out," dad commands. "Surveillance Team, stay on the house. Anything changes, advise me."

"Yes, sir," one of the other guards says

I sigh heavily as we all clear out of the house. The four of us walk to the black SUV we arrived in. Jason kicks a rock, and I growl. Ryan leans against the SUV and lets out a breath. I lean next to him and look down the hill to the house, shaking my head.

"I just don't get it," Ryan says finally, breaking the silence. "We had him. Surveillance didn't see him leave."

"Maybe he didn't." I shrug and blow out a breath.

"He wasn't in there. We all saw it. No Bird," Jason says.

18

"Maybe there's another passageway. I don't know. A secret tunnel. Another room we missed. Would we have known about that without someone telling us?" I shake my head and continue to focus down the hill.

"I think you might be right, son," dad says as he begins focusing in the same direction I am.

A movement catches my eye to the side, and I step forward. "Shit. Holy shit, he's right fucking there," I whisper pointing a couple houses down. Sure as shit, our Bird is slithering like a snake between a couple wooden fences. My entire body thrums with electric adrenaline as I take a step forward.

Ryan puts a hand on my arm. "Don't. Watch."

I shoot him a confused look, but I trust him. We wait until the Bird has disappeared between a couple houses before dad makes a move. He signals us to follow, and we all do so as silently as possible with our weapons drawn. When we get close to the houses, we catch a glimpse of him squatting down in some overgrown bushes. Dad signals Jason and Ryan to go around the back side of the house while we go around the side.

"Cobra two in position," Ryan whispers as dad and I crouch and hide out of sight of the Bird.

"Hit from behind. We'll come in from the side. Watch for crossfire. On my count," dad whispers. "Three... Two... One... Go!"

Like a well-oiled train, we all stealthily converge on the Bird. He sees me and dad and immediately pops up from his hiding place. He turns and takes off running. Unfortunately for him, he runs directly into my brothers.

I can't help but laugh. "You fucking idiot."

"Did you think for a moment you could run from us after what you did?" dad asks the Bird.

The Bird bursts out crying as he sinks to his knees, knowing the end is near for him. He covers his face in his hands. "I'm sorry! I'm so sorry!"

"Shut-up," Ryan growls. "You're pissing me off. Get up and face this like a man. If I have to drag you back to the SUV, I'm gonna fuck you up."

I look up when a light comes on upstairs in one of the houses. "We need to go. Now."

Dad follows my gaze and jerks the Bird to his feet. "Up. Scream, and I'll shoot you dead." Dad drags the Bird to the SUV and throws him in the back while me, Jason, and Ryan keep a lookout on all of the houses.

"Cobra two to all teams. The Bird is secure. Clean up and clear out."

"Yes, sir," one of our team members says.

"Good job, son. Nice catch on seeing him. It's pretty dark out. I can't say I would've seen him if I hadn't been following your gaze," dad says as he claps me on the back.

I smile at the praise. "Thank you." I slide in on one side of the Bird as Jason slides in on the other. Ryan jumps in the driver's seat as dad climbs in next to him. The Bird whimpers as we close the doors. "Let's head to the boathouse. It's closer, and we don't need to worry about waking mom."

"Good thinking, bro," Ryan says, shooting me a wink over his shoulder.

Being born to a law-abiding family who never did anything wrong, but sometimes not having enough food to eat, and then being taken in by a powerful family who makes all of their money on illegal businesses and criminal activity is something I still find completely ironic.

I came from a very poor family from the wrong side of Manhattan. My parents never really gave me much attention. I was looked at like the reason things sucked so much for us. We were lucky we didn't get shot sleeping in our beds at night. Or… at least I'm lucky I didn't get shot sleeping in my bed. My parents. They weren't so lucky.

When I was ten years old, my parents were killed in our apartment. The apartment was ransacked. I'm still not sure how I survived. I woke up when I heard our door being busted in. I ran to my closet and hid underneath a pile of clothes in the corner.

I believe in fate and miracles because of that day. Whoever killed my parents searched the house afterwards. They threw clothes and toys all over my room, even from the closet. They came close, but they never found me.

I stayed underneath that pile for hours. I didn't even come out when the police showed up. I was too scared. When I finally did come out, I packed up a backpack full of as much food as we had that wouldn't spoil on me and another one full of clothes.

I ran. I didn't get far. I was only a kid. I slept the first couple of nights in an alley near a restaurant behind a dumpster. One night, the restaurant owner saw me. He chased me out. Called the police. I ran again. I found a group of homeless people living near an overpass. I did my best to blend in amongst them. Most thought I belonged to someone.

Except Joe. He knew I didn't belong there. He looked out for me. For six months, he had become the only family I had. He taught me how to survive. He taught me how to ration my food. He taught me how to hide.

Our homeless camp was ransacked one night, though. Drug dealers who wanted the territory, but not us. For the second time in my life, I hid. I watched everyone I had become close to, including Joe, killed that night while I hid.

It was also that night that Ethan Crane showed up with what I looked at as my saving grace. I was the only survivor. He took me in. Ryan and Jason both accepted me as one of their own. Jenny looked at me like a third son. Overnight, I suddenly had a family. A family who not only provided for me, but loved me and accepted me.

I was raised just like Jason and Ryan. I went to private school. I got a trust fund. I grew up the son of a mafia boss. Strange as fuck considering where I started, but something I'll never be upset over. I regret nothing. I've not only been taught that I'm worthy of love, but also found a strength I never knew I had. I'll never hide again. I'll never have to.

"Hey, you with me over there?" Jason asks.

I jerk my head a little and clear my throat. "Yeah. I'm here."

"Good. Ready to do this?"

I nod and open my door as Ryan stops. I drag the Bird out and throw him to the ground. "We know about the drugs. Tell me about the girl."

The Bird cries as my dad and brothers encircle him. "I… can't…"

I kick him hard in the face, and then kneel next to him as he screams. "You have a sex trade ring going on?"

He nods. "I'm sorry! It was more money for my gang!"

Jason laughs. "You really aren't all that tough, are you? It's all just fun and games for you until the real challenge comes. Then you just run and hide like a…" He chuckles. "Like a little bird."

"Where're the rest of the girls?" dad asks.

"In a secret room in the house, okay? Please let me go! I'll leave town!"

Ryan kicks him hard in the face again. He screams and spits out blood into the rocks. "Where… is… the… room?" Ryan asks slowly and deliberately through gritted teeth.

"The library! The library. The wall with no books pushes open. They're there. Please let me -"

Jason shoots him. He may not be as okay with killing bad guys like the rest of us, but not even he can stand shit like a sex trade. He turns and calls a clean-up crew to deal with the mess as we all jump back in the SUV.

"We should call the police. Give them the intel," Ryan says as he starts backing the SUV up.

"And have them come after us? Will you never learn?" dad asks, disappointed.

"We could do it anonymously."

"Ryan. Please. We'll go back and release them. That's as far as we go."

"Where are they going to go, dad? We need to give them a fighting chance."

Dad sighs. "Fine. We'll do it your way. We'll release them. We call the police, and we leave. We all wear masks. We don't need to be fucking identified."

I smile a little. Ryan may have no problems taking care of the bad guys, but he has a heart of gold. Dad won't admit it, but Ryan gets that from him. We all do. None of us would be able to live with ourselves if we didn't help those who needed to be helped while protecting those who need to be protected. It's what makes us so great as a family and as a mafia. I'm lucky and grateful every damn day to be a part of both.

Chapter Four

☒ Ryan ☒

(One Year Later)

"Mr. Crane, more salt. Less sugar. I think you got them confused," my instructor says to me as she tastes my awful attempt at a croissant. I took Jason's advice and started at ICE as soon as they accepted me.

I look at the small, frail, woman with as much of an apology as I can muster. She reminds me of my grandmother. Well, when she was alive. A sweet innocent woman. Until we pissed her off. Then we had better fucking watch out. She'd chase us around the house with a broom telling us what terrible brats we were. I chuckle despite myself. She wasn't wrong.

I look down in frustration at the ingredients in front of me and glare at the sugar. I had to have switched the two. My miserable excuse for a croissant is nothing like I'm used to. I taught my mother how to make croissants. I shouldn't have an issue making them. What the fuck is wrong with me?

"I think that's the first mistake I've ever seen you make," the girl next to me whispers. I glance down at her. I can't say she's not gorgeous.

It's been fun flirting with her all year. A man could drown in her emerald eyes and get lost in her luscious blonde locks.

I reach up and twist some of her hair around my finger and tug. The small moan that escapes her lips every time I do it is the reason I've done it a few hundred times. Why she hasn't ended up in my bed yet is something I can't figure out. It's not for a lack of trying on my part.

"I'm starting to think the reason I like you so much is because you've been holding out on me. Most women would have been falling over themselves to be with me."

She gives me a sexy smile. "And because I haven't makes you fall over yourself for me."

I drop my hand with a small smirk. "I've never fallen all over myself to be with anyone." I intentionally let my eyes wander all over her body. She shivers. "You won't be the exception."

She licks her bottom lip as she turns back to her station. "Don't confuse the sugar for salt in your croissants this time, Crane."

I laugh as I concentrate on the ingredients. When I put them in the oven, I take out my phone and see a text from my dad. I sigh heavily and contemplate putting my phone back in my pocket. Unfortunately for me, I'm too loyal of a fucking son. Maybe I need to become more of an asshole. I glare at my phone and open the text.

> **Ethan: New threat on the horizon. Got word these guys are growing and spilling into our territory downtown. Need all three of you tonight. No exceptions.**

I stare at my phone in utter annoyance before I type a furious reply.

> **Ryan: You know I can't! I have finals. We all have finals!**

I fight the urge to slam my phone on the counter. I love my father. We all do. But I swear. Even though he says he'd never force us to help, he's sure trying to sabotage us. All of us. He has to know that none of us are fucking superheroes. No one can keep up with the schedule he makes us keep!

> **Ethan: Sure. I'll just take people who aren't as good as you. Maybe I won't get my ass killed. I need you and your brothers.**
> **Ryan: No. Dad, we have finals. We can't keep this up. Nick is going to get kicked out of school because his fucking grades are so low since you make us go out almost every night.**

Ethan: I just saw his report card. He's not failing anything.

I stare at my phone incredulously before growling low under my throat.

Ryan: Dad, Nick is a straight A student! He's been getting C's this entire year! His professors think he's on drugs!

Ethan: You can't see it, but I'm seething. What is wrong with you?

Ryan: Me? What's wrong with you? You've never made us go if we felt like we couldn't, or if we were falling behind. What the fuck aren't you telling me, old man?

Ethan: I will not get into that over the fucking text.

Ryan: Over the fucking text? Do you speak English? Forget it. We aren't going. I talked to Jason and Nick. We all voted. We aren't going. And if you try to make us, I'll go to mom.

Ethan: Don't you threaten me with your mother, you insolent prick.

I choke down the laugh attempting to bubble up from my throat at my dad's attempt at humor and insult. I've learned a lot from him. Humor and insults wasn't one of them. But I can't deny it isn't funny when he tries.

Ryan: Dad, I don't mean to be an asshole, but we can't do it. Nick has to study, or he's going to fail. I just put sugar instead of salt in my croissants because I'm so fucking tired I can't think straight. Even Jas is struggling. We need to focus, or we'll all have to repeat this year.

I put my phone back in my pocket as the oven dings. I pull out my croissants, and my mouth waters at the smell.

Much better. So much fucking better.

I put them on the cooling rack to cool and lean down on my elbows. There's no way we can help tonight. There's no way we can help the rest of the semester. We all need to focus.

Standing up to my dad has never been easy. I typically don't have to do it. He's always been respectful of me and my brothers. If we don't want to go on a mission, he usually doesn't make us.

The problem is that over this past year since we took out that sex trade ring, he's been on a mission. A mission that he's kept me in the dark about. Very strange. He never keeps me in the dark about anything. He's

25

always said since I'm taking over for him, I need to know everything. Despite that, we've always been an open family. We don't keep secrets. Secrets, just like assumptions, can get us killed.

I sigh and glance at the girl next to me. "Mia, can I ask you something?"

"Sure." She breaks one of her croissants in half and blows on it.

"Say your family expects you to take over the family company, but you have other directions you want to take the company. You know the company will be far more successful if you go ahead with your plans. The problem is, your family won't let you take the company in the direction you want to. What do you do?"

Mia takes a bite of the croissant and crinkles her nose as she drops it on the counter. "Gross."

I pick up one of her croissants and taste it. "You didn't add any sugar." I put the rest of the croissant on the counter as she grabs one of mine.

She takes a bite and moans quietly. "So much better."

I shake my head and chuckle. "I'm being serious. Help me out here."

She finishes the croissant as she watches me. Finally, she sighs. "Can I ask you something?"

I shrug. "Go ahead."

"You're taking over the Crane Mafia from your father. What is it that you're so afraid of after you take over? If you want to take it in a different direction, who's going to stop you? Your father?"

"I never said anything about a mafia."

"Everyone knows who you are. Everyone knows who Ethan Crane is. He runs one of the most powerful mafias in the world. My dad's the police commissioner. Even he won't go up against your father."

I chuckle. "It's a cross I bear, I guess."

"Ryan, the point is you can't be afraid of *after* you take over." She shrugs. "It's yours. You'll face backlash. Your dad might be mad, but I've known you for a while now. I know how close you are to your brothers. That has to come from somewhere, and my bet is your father."

I smile. "My family is close. My dad's kind of on a warpath, but yeah. We're all still close."

"He might get mad, but he'll support you."

The teacher starts coming around to taste everyone's second attempt at croissants, and Mia wipes away a tear. I raise an eyebrow. "What's wrong?"

"I'm going to fail. If I fail this, it won't matter if I ace the final. I don't know why I even bother. I want to be a chef and own my own restaurant someday. It's been my dream since I could walk. Obviously, I suck at it."

I glance back as the teacher makes her way back to us one by one. When the teacher has her back to us, I quickly throw all of Mia's croissants away as her eyes widen in shock. "Ryan! What are you doing?" she hisses as her eyes dart to the front of the room to the teacher.

I wink at her and put some of mine on her cooling rack. "You have talent. I'm not letting you fail."

Her eyes shine with unshed tears as she realizes the kindness I'm showing her. "Thank you," she whispers.

"Don't thank me. Just don't flunk out. I'm looking forward to visiting your restaurant."

She nods as we wait for the teacher to make her way back to us. "I really don't know what to say, Ryan."

"Don't say anything."

The teacher gives us both a passing grade with a very happy smile and glowing praise of our croissants. Mia holds herself together until we're dismissed from class before she gathers her belongings and tugs me by the hand with her. I follow with an amused smile as she leads me directly to my car.

Letting go of my hand, she heads to the passenger side and waits for me to unlock the door before she climbs in. "Just drive. Anywhere private."

I slowly get behind the wheel and start the engine, keeping one eye on her. "Why, exactly?"

"Because I'm finally going to give you what you've been wanting this entire year. As a thank you."

I laugh and shake my head as I drive out of my parking place. I never park in a manner that would force me to have to back out of the spot in case I need to leave quickly. "No. I'm not doing that just because you think it's a good way to thank me."

She looks at me a little confused. "Y-you don't want me?"

27

I look over at her as I stop at a light. "I do want you. Just not like that. Even I have morals."

She rubs her legs together and shifts a little. Her skirt rides up her thighs. I bite my lip and start driving. She shifts again and crosses her legs, whimpering a little as she tries to focus on the cars I'm passing as I drive. She uncrosses her legs, but clenches them tightly together.

I groan as I drop a hand on her thigh. She looks at me and bites her lip as I pull her leg a little so she unclenches. She inhales sharply and lets her legs fall open. I slide my hand under her skirt to her pussy. I cup it and give it a few rubs and squeezes.

She moans and drops her head back against the seat. "Mmm... Please, Ryan. I've been so wet for you all class." She looks at me through hooded eyes. "I've never thrown myself at anyone before, but I don't think I can survive anymore flirting and touching and back and forth between us. I can't hold out anymore."

I give her a sexy smile as I slide her panties aside and slide my middle finger inside her. She jerks and arches into me. "I can't let you go on being all uncomfortable in a car like this."

"Oh!"

I thrust my finger into her deeply and slide it all the way out before pushing it as far into her as it will go. I give her hard, deep thrusts as I expertly steer through the traffic. She grips the seat as she spreads her legs wider, giving me easier access. I give her a second finger and continue with the hard, deep thrusts, as I quicken my pace. She tightens and clenches tight around me as she comes.

"You weren't kidding, were you? You really have been wanting that. Should have told me you were that close. I would've helped you out in class." I glance at her with a cocky half smile.

"Mmm... Ryan..." She holds my wrist as she clenches her legs together while she comes.

I thrust my fingers slowly until I feel her orgasm slow. She relaxes more and more as each second passes. She loosens her grip on my wrist, and I pull out of her gently. I put my fingers up to her mouth. Her eyes widen, and she glances at me.

"Suck them. You can't tell me you've never tasted yourself."

28

"U-um…" She takes a tentative lick, and I chuckle at her utter embarrassment but don't move my fingers. Finally, she takes them both into her mouth and moans while she licks and sucks herself off of them.

"There we go. That's what I wanted." I slowly take my fingers out of her mouth and answer the phone as it starts ringing. I put it on speaker. "What?"

"Did you tell your father no to helping him tonight?" my mother's angry voice fills the car.

"Mom, we have finals. You both know that."

"Ryan Nathanial Crane! Get home. Now!" Mom leaves no room for argument as she hangs up.

I sigh and reluctantly turn off an exit to head back to the school. "I'm sorry, Mia."

"Hey. Family. I get it. My house is actually close to here. I can take a LYFT to school tomorrow if you want to drop me off."

"I'll pick you up. Don't be ridiculous."

She chuckles. "I know you don't date, Crane. Picking me up for school is kind of a dating thing. I can get there on my own."

"I don't date anyone, but I can still pick you up and bring you to school considering I can't give you what we both want right now. I don't live that far from here anyway. You're on the way."

"I'll just look forward to sex with the amazing Ryan Crane another day. See if you're all they say you are."

I laugh. "All who says I am? The tabloids?"

She gives me a sexy smile. "Well…, them, too."

I laugh again. "I assure you," I begin. I glance at her and wink. "I'm far better."

She gives me a sexy smile and licks her lips. She clenches her thighs together again and quickly looks away. I reach over and finger her a second time as she directs me to her house. It's the least I can do since I don't have the time to fuck her. I'm too much of a gentleman to leave her needy and wet for me like that.

She comes with a scream. Her body shakes and trembles as she uncontrollably twitches and jerks while her pussy pulses softly around my fingers. I slowly pull my fingers out and suck her off of them while she straightens out her clothing. Her cheeks flush a pretty shade of pink.

After I drop her off, I reluctantly head home. I don't know what's going on, but if my mother is pissed that I told dad we aren't helping him tonight, I know something big is happening. My stomach clenches, and my heart races the closer I get to the house. I rub my temple to ease the sudden headache as I try to figure out what the fuck my father has gotten us into.

I know instinctively that I need to know. I hate that I may have to force him to tell me.

Chapter Five

☒ Jason ☒

I pace nervously in the family room waiting for the tell-tale sign of Ryan's Ferrari. I've been growing increasingly more restless and nervous as the days go on. I've never seen my father so tense. Him being tense makes all of us tense, but we're usually okay unless Ryan feels it. If Ryan feels it, we all get nervous. Ryan has always been the calm one in the face of any storm.

"Jas, if you don't stop pacing, you might start a fire," Nick grumbles from the corner.

I force a steady breath and look at him. "Something major is going on. You know it as well as I do. Dad's been tense, but Ryan's been..." I trail off and shrug.

"He's been tired. We all have been."

"It's more than that. Ryan has been on edge. You know how cool and collected he is. Even he's been jumpy."

"Exhaustion does fucked up things to people."

I shake my head. "You know better."

He sighs and stands. "Yeah. Something is wrong. But it's not going to do anyone any good if you or I start freaking out about it. We need to know what it is."

"You think Ryan knows?"

He shakes his head. "No. Ryan doesn't keep anything from us even if dad tells him to keep it quiet."

"So you think Ryan is just as in the dark as us?"

"Not a doubt in my mind."

I nod and start pacing again just as I hear Ryan pull into the driveway. "Fuck. Finally."

"Jason, you have to relax, man. Whatever it is, we'll get through it as a family like we always do."

Ryan walks through the door on his cell phone and motions for me and Nick to follow. "I said it, didn't I? I'll be there at five to sign the papers." He leads us into our dad's office. I glance at Nick. He shoots me a confused look and shrugs. "My last name doesn't do it for you? Come on." He sits across from our dad. Nick and I follow and both shrug at dad when he shoots us a questioning look. "Good. See you at five." Ryan hangs up and grins like a fool.

Dad rubs his temple. "What did you buy now?"

"A jet."

All of our mouths fall open. It's dad who recovers the quickest. "Are you trying to give me a heart attack, or does it come naturally?"

Ryan's grin widens. "It comes naturally."

"You're lucky you're my son. If I didn't love you, I'd shoot you."

I laugh. "Even you aren't a cold-blooded killer, dad."

He glares, but we all see the smile. "Down to business. We have a new threat, and it's unlike anything I've seen. At least not for a long time."

"How long have you known and not told me?" Ryan asks.

Dad sighs. "A while. I've been running surveillance and gathering intel."

We all look at each other before looking back at him. I take a deep breath. "Who is it? Why all the secrecy?"

Dad looks at me, then down at his hands. "Because this threat… It's… big. They're a growing mafia. They're… close to us in size and power."

"What?" Nick asks incredulously. "Dad, how could you keep that from us?"

Ryan stands and paces as he runs his fingers through his hair. "You've never kept me in the dark before. Any of us. Even if you thought it was small and insignificant and they didn't need to know. You knew I'd tell them anyway. We don't keep secrets. You taught us that. Why now?"

"To protect my family. I needed information. That's why I've had you go on so many of these smaller missions. I needed to be free and available if I needed to be, but these other smaller deals needed to be done."

Ryan collapses in a chair and lets out a huff. "Ridiculous. You've been running us into the ground, dad. And now you expect us to be alert and ready to go tonight to take down a band of assholes that are just as big and just as powerful as we are? You're fucking insane."

"I didn't have a choice, Ryan."

"Right," Ryan growls.

"Stop it. Everyone just stop it," I say holding up a hand. "None of that helps us now. We need to figure out tonight. Obviously, we're all tired."

"There's no way we can go out and participate in this," Nick says, rubbing his head. "I have a perpetual headache that won't go away. One of my professors told me that if I fail another quiz, I'll fail the class."

"If I get a single question wrong on my final, I'll fail," I say. "We have to figure this out."

"We can't just leave him hanging. I'll go," Ryan says, defeated, as he stands. "I need to go take a fucking nap."

"Ryan, wait," Nick says. "I owe this family everything. I'll go. You and Jason focus on school."

"No. Your grades and Jason's are lower than mine. I'll work it out." Ryan leaves the room, and dad slumps in his chair.

"Dad," I start. I don't like going up against my father of all people, but I know Ryan. He's been conditioned to believe nothing is more important than this mafia. He's accepted this is his destiny long ago. I don't doubt he wants to take over. Ryan has big plans for our mafia. None of which he's going to be able to do if he keeps putting it above himself, and his own damn needs. "He's just as fucking wiped out as us. He's not going to be his best. None of us are."

33

"I'm starting to see that, son." Dad sighs and wipes his hands down his face. "I'll get a team together. I'll have to take Lorenzo and maybe Blake. I'm sorry, boys. I really thought you all just wanted a Friday night to yourselves."

Nick shakes his head. "We've been on missions almost every single day this entire month. We can't do this and sustain our schedule at school. It's not feasible."

Dad nods. "I know. I understand now. We'll make it work."

I let out a relieved breath. "So... who's this mafia?"

"It's the Lucinio Mafia. They're based out of Los Angeles. They have a few factions in the bigger cities like we do, but they haven't bothered us."

"Why now?" Nick questions.

"I don't know. My intel says they've taken territories we aren't in, but the person leading now has decided to expand. I guess he's been leading for a while, but the previous leader still had quite the hold. Now that he's gone, the new leader is taking things in a different direction. They aren't as new as I said, but they are a lot bigger now. That's what's making them seem so new."

I chuckle. "So, they've decided to take over territory from a powerful mafia that everyone knows something about? Must have a death wish."

"I don't think that's the game here. I think their plan is to expand, and I think they believe they can take us. My sources say they've grown over the past few years exponentially. It's quite possible they've been lying in wait. Just waiting for the perfect moment to attack us."

"It seems to have shaken you," Nick says.

"I won't lie to you. It's scary. Truly scary. I've never come up against someone as big as me. Your grandfather and great-grandfather are to thank for getting us to the point we are. I've spent most of my life maintaining this. I never anticipated the need to expand. I thought we were untouchable. I was wrong."

"Is there a way to do this mission tomorrow? Give us a day to recoup?" Nick asks

"No. I'm sorry, but no. We have an opportunity. You boys know better than anyone that when we have an opportunity, we need to take it. We may not get another chance." Dad looks sadly down at his desk a moment before he stands. "I'm sorry I refused to see what this was doing to you boys. I've been focused on one thing and one thing only, and I've ignored how it's affecting you. I won't make that mistake again."

I look at him as Nick and I both stand. "You know now. You understand. That's what matters. What's the plan now?"

"The plan is that you boys rest and concentrate on your studies. I'll get the best of who we have, and we'll strike tonight like we planned."

Nick chews on his lip and looks at us both with concern. "Are you sure? If this Lucinio Mafia is as big as you say, you need to know that those out there have your back. You always feel safer if you have family out there."

"This mafia is family. You know that, son." Dad claps Nick and me both on the back and walks towards the door of his office. "I need to talk to Ryan. I probably owe him a bigger apology than I owe the both of you. I've been pretty hard on him."

"He's tough, dad. He can take it," I say with a soft smile. Dad nods as Nick and I head for the stairs. We don't say a word until we get to the top. "I don't know whether to sleep or study."

"Sleep. The answer is sleep. I've gotten six hours in three days. I'm not sure how I'm still standing."

"Lucky that final for your criminal class isn't tomorrow."

"Thank fuck for that. I'm dead on my feet."

I glance at my door before looking back at Nick. "Hey, about Penelope."

He shakes his head and holds up a hand. "Don't. Don't start. I'm asking her to marry me. We've been together for four years now. We know how we feel about each other and that's all that matters, Jas."

"I know. I get it. I don't agree, but you know that. I'm just… about the account."

"Jason, she'll be on it eventually."

"But why now?"

"Because we're getting married."

"Nick." I close my eyes and pinch the bridge of my nose. He puts a hand on my arm.

"I know you don't trust her. I know Ryan doesn't. But I know her. I've been with her for a long time. I trust her. She's not a gold-digger. She isn't going to clean me out."

I open my eyes and look him directly in his. "I really think you need to hold off on giving her access to your accounts. You have access to part of your trust fund now. That means so will she."

"Please trust me. Penelope isn't going to fuck me over. Just because you guys don't like her doesn't mean she isn't a good person."

"She's always talking about the stuff you do for her. The dinners. The trips at the end of the semester. Things you buy her. Nick, open your eyes. You're miserable with her."

"No. I'm not. She makes me feel like a real person. Sometimes, I feel like this larger-than-life character in some weird movie about a life I don't even belong in. She grounds me. Penelope is my way of making sure I don't become some vicious killer."

"You'd never do that."

"Wouldn't I? I don't feel anything when I shoot someone. I turn all emotions off and put it in the back of my mind. I can't say I enjoy it. That would make me a sociopath. I'm not. But I don't feel anything. Dad could tell me right now to shoot someone. I wouldn't even question it. I'd do it. Not only because I trust him, but because I don't feel anything. Penelope makes me feel. Can't you understand that?"

"Nick, I understand that part of it, but that doesn't mean you shouldn't protect yourself. You shouldn't give her access to your accounts. You don't know. Set up something for the both of you that's separate. I know you don't think she's capable of it, but you have to watch your back."

"She might piss you and Ryan off, Jason, but she's a good person. She wouldn't hurt me like that. It's not in her nature."

I try to hold down my frustration, but it's obvious my brother is blinded by whatever spell she cast on him. He can't, and refuses to, see her for her true colors. It's easier to catch it if you aren't involved, but I hate the fact that he won't listen. I know she's going to hurt him. I can sense it, and I'm not the only one. Everyone can see it, but no one will approach Nick.

"Look. Everyone says you need to learn the lesson for yourself. I'm the only one who's trying to make you see it. Just think more about it."

He sighs. "Fine. I'll think more about it." He looks longingly at his room. "I need sleep."

I nod. "Me, too." He stalks off to his room, and I enter mine with a yawn. I glance at him as he shuts himself in his room. I close my door and fall, exhausted, onto my bed. I don't have the foggiest idea what I'm thinking as I drift into a hard, much-needed sleep.

Chapter Six

⚔ Nick ⚔

(One Month Later)

My heart is racing. I haven't felt this scared since my parents were killed. I can't breathe. Everything is telling me to run.

Instead, I force myself to take a few deep breaths and focus. I inhale the fresh May air. I let myself relax into the grass I'm lying in. I close my eyes and let the sun warm me. My blood eventually stops humming in my ears, and my heart begins to slow.

Next to me, Penelope hums softly to herself as she picks the pedals off a flower. I open my eyes and watch her. She's so beautiful. Her gorgeous, red hair falls in waves down her shoulders and cascades down her back. Her emerald green eyes catch the sunlight, and golden sparkles dance across their depths.

I reach up and softly brush my fingers across her creamy, silky skin. "You're so beautiful, Nel."

She looks down at me with a soft smile before abandoning the flower and cuddling into my side. "You say that all the time. I never get sick of it." She smiles a bright smile, and her eyes crinkle as she bites her lip. I reach up and run my fingers through her satiny locks. She pulls away with a teasing smile. "Do you know how long it takes me to get my hair to look good for you?"

"I don't care. You're beautiful just the way you are. You don't need to spend so much time glamming up."

"And look like a slug on the arm of one of the richest men in the world? I don't think so."

"Does the money really matter that much?"

"Of course not, baby. But I don't want to make you look bad."

"That's not possible. You're what makes me look so good."

She laughs quietly as I run my thumb across her lips. I lean forward to kiss her. When our lips meet, the familiar fire that always starts low in my stomach ignites. I part her lips slightly with my tongue before deepening it and diving in. As she always does, she melts into me, though a little reserved. I slide my hand up and down her back before resting it on her ass and pulling her closer to me.

"Nick," she moans. I love how needy and hot she gets for me so quickly. She presses against me and grips my shirt. Her tits hit my chest, and I groan. I grip her ass tighter before realizing where we are.

I pull back a little and tug her hair to bring her back to reality. "We're in the middle of Central Park, honey."

She bites her lip, and her cheeks redden. "Sorry. I always get a little carried away when it comes to you."

I smile as we sit up. "Same here. It's been that way ever since we met."

She beams shyly at me before focusing on the spread in front of us. "So… what's all this?"

I pop the cork on her favorite chardonnay. "I thought we could celebrate. Our first year of college is done." I pour us each a glass and hand her hers. She takes it with a soft smile and digs into the grapes and cheese assortment I brought.

"I can't think of a better way to celebrate." She takes a sip of her wine, and I take a sip of mine to hide my smile. Digging a hole in my pocket is a one karat diamond ring on a yellow gold band. I've been waiting for the perfect moment to give it to her. I think I found it.

I reach into my pocket and take out the ring. "I might be able to think of a better way." I shift and drop to one knee. She stares at me wide-eyed with her wine glass halfway to her mouth.

"Are you…?"

"Penelope, I love you. I've been in love with you since we first met. I think you felt the same. I trust you implicitly. I'm glad I can always be myself around you and not what everyone sees me as. You're such a caring, passionate woman. You know I want to spend the rest of my life with you. Will you marry me?"

She nods as her eyes fill with tears. She throws her arms around me. "Yes! Oh my God, yes! Yes!"

I wrap her in my arms and kiss her neck as I breathe a sigh of relief. "I really thought you were going to say no."

She pulls away and looks in my eyes. "Are you kidding? Why would you think that?"

I shrug. "I'm from the ghetto, Nel. You're way out of my league. I've never forgotten how lucky I am."

"You are lucky. But so am I. I'm lucky to have a man willing to take care of me and get me out of the hellhole I live in."

I smile and tug her down onto the blanket next to me as she admires her ring. Penelope may have had a worse life than me. She didn't grow up poor. She never had to worry about food. Her parents got her anything she wanted. The problem was they were never there for her. I know all too well how that feels. No matter how close I've become with my Crane family, the scars left by my parents when I was a kid never really disappeared. Every time I look at Penelope and how hurt she gets when her parents jet off to some far away land, my own wounds open up.

"You'll always have me."

"I'm counting on it," she says softly against my chest. We stay in the park wrapped in each other's arms until the sun starts to set. Penelope looks up at me. "It's so pretty. You should've asked me now to marry you. It would've been perfect."

I chuckle and kiss the top of her head. "It felt right."

"Maybe we could stage something. You know. For the media."

"Why would we do that? I hate the media. My whole family does."

"Well, they love you and your family. One of the Crane brothers off the market is really big news."

I sigh and sit up, letting her go. "Nel, we try to stay out of the media. They tend to find us and snap their pictures, but we don't seek them out. You know that."

She bites her lip and sighs as she sits up and starts gathering everything together, getting ready to leave. "I thought it would be good publicity considering how your family is never really getting that."

"We don't care, Nel. That's why the media and tabloids like us so much. They can make up anything they want to, and we never respond."

"I still don't get it. Why allow them to trash you?"

"Because we don't care about them. We know who we are."

"Most mafia families tend to try and make themselves look good."

I shrug and stand as she finishes gathering everything. I help her up and then bend to grab the blanket and fold it. "We aren't most mafias."

She shakes her head as we walk to my car. After we get everything packed away and settled, I take off, heading home. We drive in silence until I pull into my driveway. After I park in the garage, Penelope looks at me.

"Don't you think good publicity is a good idea?"

"I really don't care one way or the other."

"Then let me plan something for the press." Her eyes light up when I glance at her. "Please? You could propose at sunset."

"I already proposed." I take her hand and hold her ring finger up. "See?"

She laughs. "You could propose every day, and I'd still love it."

I laugh as I get out of the car. "Once was enough. I don't know how the words came out. I was nervous as fuck."

She takes my hand as we walk in the house. She holds her ring up, admiring it again. I can't help but swell with pride at how much she loves it. I glance around the house and usher Penelope upstairs. I don't want to face my family right now. All I want is her. Touching and petting and her rubbing against me has me so far off the deep end I can't think of anything but her underneath me.

"What's the hurry?" she giggles, and the sound goes straight to my cock. I glance over my shoulder and open the door, impatiently pulling her inside. Seconds later, I have her pushed up against the door with my tongue in her mouth, and my hands on her tits.

I groan into her mouth. "Fuck, I've wanted this all day."

41

"Mmm…" Her hand finds my cock. She rubs and squeezes it, and I nearly come in my jeans.

"Don't, baby. You don't know how close I am." She keeps rubbing and squeezing and my eyes roll back in my head. I take a step back to catch my breath and gain control over myself.

She whimpers and pouts as she looks up at me through her lashes. "Nick…"

I smile devilishly as I tug her to the bed. She giggles and bites her lip. I love when she plays shy. I know better than anyone that she isn't shy at all. My point is proven when she starts stripping me of my clothes as soon as we reach my bed.

I groan when she drops to her knees, tugging my pants and underwear down with her. She takes my cock in her mouth and starts sucking hard and fast as she bobs her head up and down. She licks my tip and tugs on my balls before she deep-throats me and swallows. And just like that she has me coming, my hot liquid spilling down the back of her throat.

"Damn, I'll never understand how you do that so fast." I tug her up by her hair after she finishes licking me clean. My rock-hard cock hasn't come close to being spent for the day. I need to feel myself inside her. I reach for a condom as she strips the rest of her clothes.

"Nick," she whines. "We're engaged to be married. Why do you insist on wearing a condom?"

I pause a second and shoot her a look as my heart starts pounding. Ryan and Jason are always warning me about the need for condoms when it comes to relationships. They're always saying how women take advantage of men in positions of power like we are. How they try to trick us.

"Because I don't want kids right now, Nel," I say as I put the condom on. It's not a lie, but it's also the only thing I can think of to appease her. "Why would you even say that? We may be getting married, but neither of us want kids now. We still have to get through college."

She shrugs, and I raise a suspicious eyebrow. "I guess I didn't really think of that. You're right."

She finishes taking off her clothes. I forget everything we were talking about when I see her standing there in all her glory. She crawls into the bed and wiggles her ass for me. I smack it and crawl in after her, tugging her on top of me. In a single thrust, I finally get what my body craves.

Her.

"Jesus, I need this." I start thrusting into her as she wraps her legs around me. She tries to sit up, but that's not how I want her. I grip her tightly and flip her onto her back without pulling out. I pin her to the bed and continue thrusting.

"Oh, yes!" She claws at my back.

I reach for both of her hands and pin them over her head holding her wrists. She's always trying to scratch and bite me. It's like she's trying to mark her territory, even though I've repeatedly told her to knock it off. Walking around with bite marks and scratches earns me nothing but ridicule from my brothers.

I bend to kiss her neck as I start quickening my pace. My smooth thrusts become more frantic and harder with every push into her sweet, wet pussy. Every sexy moan that comes out of her mouth, or guttural growl that comes from deep within her stomach, makes me impossibly harder for her. Every time she meets my thrusts makes me drive into her deeper and faster until I'm slamming into her just as hard as she's pushing against my hips. My balls spank her pussy. I nip her neck and suck. She pulls away from me while still pounding herself against me.

"You know I hate hickies." She attempts to pull her wrists free, but I keep them gripped firmly in my hand. She tries uselessly to pull away and weakens as her pussy clenches around me. She comes with a sigh, and I drop my head on the pillow. She tightens and pulses around me.

I groan. "I wasn't there yet."

"I always wait for you. I couldn't anymore. Besides, you already came." She pushes me off her as soon as I let go of her wrists and heads directly for the bathroom. I roll over onto my back and yank the condom off, frustrated beyond belief.

Maybe I did jump the gun. Being nineteen and engaged to be married doesn't seem like the best idea. I glance at the picture of the two of us on my nightstand as I toss the condom in the garbage. We'd just met. I'm giving her a piggy-back ride through the garden behind our house. We're both laughing and look like we don't have a care in the world. Mom snapped it when we didn't notice.

43

I smile at the memory. That and so many other memories. That's how I know she's the one for me. My family may not agree, but she's always understood me far better than so many others, except Jason and Ryan.

That picture. It's how I know I'm making the right decision. Consequences with my family be damned.

Chapter Seven

⚔ Ryan ⚔

(One Year Later)

"This is even more stupid than the jet and the house," Nick says to me.

I shrug. "It's Hawaii. Who wouldn't want a mansion in Hawaii?"

"Dad is going to kill you," Jason says, shaking his head at the paperwork and images of the pristine mansion on the cliffs of Maui. Sleek. Sophisticated.

"It even has a helipad for my new chopper." I smile and wink.

"Ryan, you blew your entire inheritance on frivolous shit." Nick paces the dining room.

"How the fuck are we going to keep this from dad?" Jason stands and moves to the window that overlooks the garden.

I sigh. "It's my inheritance. And it's not your responsibility to protect me. I can handle our father."

Nick and Jason look at each other before looking back at me. Jason shakes his head. "Dad was pissed about the house here. How the hell do you think he's going to take a house in Hawaii?"

"It's not his decision. It's mine. I'm twenty-two years old. He can't expect I'll live here forever. We have a lot of business in Hawaii. I'd prefer to stay in my own house over some hotel."

"He's not going to take this well," Nick says. "I swear. I think you live to give that man a stroke."

I can't help but smile. "A couple years ago on the way to school, Jason gave me some great advice. He said I need to start doing things for myself. Things that make me happy."

"What? Fuck! I meant going to culinary school, you asshole! Not buy a fucking jet and two houses!"

"And the car. Don't forget the new Lamborghini," I joke.

"Right. The fucking Lamborghini. Who the fuck could forget that?" Jason huffs. "Why can't you invest like normal people?"

"Invest? You mean like you did? I don't think you used your inheritance for anything fun." One of my greatest joys in life is egging Jason on and pissing my father off. Both give me reactions that warm the dark, cold corners of my heart.

"Some of us have a plan for our future," Jason grumbles.

"I have a plan for the future. Just don't intend on starting that future now. I plan to live a little first."

"Unbelievable." Nick sits back down and rubs his temple.

"At least I didn't give Penelo-slut access to it."

"She's had access since the day after we got engaged. She hasn't taken a dime of it."

"Because you give her everything she wants," Jason interjects before I have the opportunity to say anything. "What the hell was up with that media frenzied engagement anyway?"

Nick growls low in his throat. "I told you. She wanted good publicity for the family."

I shake my head and stand, patting him on the back. "No. She wanted to flaunt her pretty boy toy in front of the entire world, and you let her."

"Asshole," Nick mumbles under his breath as I leave the room in search of our father.

Hearing him in his office, I smile and don't bother knocking as I walk in and drop on the couch. He's talking to his second in command and

46

shoots me a dirty look. I smirk and lay on the couch. I put my hands behind my head and cross my feet, making myself comfortable.

"Forgive my son. He thinks he owns the world. Apparently, I didn't raise him properly." Dad glares at me, and I grin.

"Let my wife smack him around a little. Brandy put the fear of God into our kids at a very young age," Charlie says to my dad.

"They fear Jenny. They seem to think they can push my buttons. Maybe I should have beaten them." Dad looks over and winks at me.

I grin. "Yeah. Maybe you should have taken the belt after us. Perhaps then I wouldn't have bought a house in Hawaii just to piss you off."

He blinks at me a few times before he slumps in his chair. "Why? Why Hawaii?"

"Because it's a nice getaway far away from here, and women from Hawaii are hot as fuck."

"I'm not giving you another dime. You're cut off. You can make your own way. I'm giving the damn reins to Nick."

I laugh as I sit up. "Sure. Go ahead."

"Why do you do this to me? Have I not been a good father?"

"You're a great father. But it's my personal mission to see how far I can push you before your head explodes."

"So it is fun for you. Get out."

I laugh again as I stand up. I walk behind his desk and kiss him on top of the head. "If you need me, I'll be planning a trip for me, Jason, and Nick to Hawaii. We'll take my jet."

"Insolent asshole. Get out of my office before I have Charlie shoot you."

"You love me too much." I pat him on the back and head out of the office. I don't miss the look of pure amusement all over Charlie's face.

I'll admit I've become more rebellious over the past couple of years. Ever since I decided Jason was right and I need to do things for myself instead of always doing what my dad wants, my rebellion has become far more upfront. Above and beyond buying two houses, a helicopter, a jet, and a new car, I've also refused to go on several missions.

I turn the corner to the kitchen. A body runs into me. I start to catch whoever it is, but realize it's Penelope, so I watch as she falls to the

47

ground. I don't bother trying to catch her. I cross my arms over my chest when she reaches out a hand for me to help her up.

"God, you're an asshole. You can't be bothered to help a lady up?"

I smirk and lean against the wall. "I don't see a lady. I see a little bitch who's fucking with my little brother."

She stands. "Haven't I proven myself to you and your family? I'm not after Nick's money."

"You can say that all you want, but actions speak louder than words."

"I've done nothing but spend my time loving him for who he is and trying to prove myself to you and your judgemental family. I don't know why you don't like me. You've never taken the time to even get to know me," she hisses through her overly plump and way too pink lips.

"You aren't my type. You wear way too much makeup." I look her up and down. "Slutty as fuck clothing. Oh. And you'd be after my money just like you are his."

She huffs. "I wouldn't date you anyway. You're too cocky."

I laugh. "Well, thank the my fucking lucky stars." I lean a little closer to her and whisper in her ear with a low and dangerous growl. "I wouldn't be caught dead near you." I stand to my full height and look down at her. "You need to break it off with Nick."

She glares, unfazed by my intimidation. "Why would I do anything you tell me to?"

"I don't expect you to do it." I shrug as I step closer to her. "But if you do anything to hurt him, you'll wish you never fucked with him."

I give her credit. She stands her ground. She even pokes a finger into my chest and glares up at me a little more viciously. "You... don't scare me. Just because you're the heir to the mafia doesn't give you the right to try and intimidate me."

I look down at the finger she still has against my chest before slowly looking back at her. I shoot her my own glare, and she visibly shivers. Fucking about time. I know how intimidating I can be. It's part of what makes me who I am. I'm twenty-two and not a lot of people fuck with me. Most of them know better.

"You'd best do yourself a favor. Walk away. From me. From this family. Especially from my little brother."

She takes a step closer so she's touching me with her chest, and I growl as I narrow my eyes further. She looks up at me. "What I do is none of your business. Nick gave me access to his account because he trusts me, and I haven't touched a dime. I could drain his account tomorrow, and there's not a damn thing you could do about it. Because legally, that money is just as much mine as it is his."

I don't move like she expects me to. I stand tall and shoot electric hatred from my eyes. "I'm on to you, Penelope. I may not be able to come after you legally, but I can fucking make your life a living hell if you so much as think about fucking with him."

She gives me a sickening smile and lowers her voice. "What if I told you that you couldn't touch me once I have my hands on his fortune? Not even the great Crane family can find everyone if they disappear."

She tries to shove past me, but I don't budge a single fucking millimeter. I grab her wrist and slowly move it from my chest as I squeeze and bend it slightly. Her eyes widen. It's obvious that she didn't think I'd touch her because she's a woman. To me, she's the enemy. Male or female, I'll never allow anyone to hurt my family.

"Walk... Away... Now." I drop her wrist. She bites her lip as she turns and hightails it to whatever hole of Hell she crawled out of. I let out a low groan as I shake my head.

"Well, that was enlightening," Nick's voice comes from behind me.

I turn, a little surprised, and furrow my eyebrows. "What was?"

"She literally just said once she has her hands on my fortune, we can't touch her because she'll disappear." He leans against the wall and lets out a breath as he closes his eyes and shakes his head. "I saw it. I ignored it, but I saw it. That's probably what makes me feel the most idiotic right now."

I lean against the wall next to him as he opens his eyes and looks up at me. "You're in love, Nick. I've never been in love, but I imagine it's not easy. You want to believe in the woman you love. It's not easy to look at the bigger picture and see the stuff the rest of us see."

"But I did. I've seen it for months now. I didn't want to believe it. I wanted to believe that she loved me."

"You see it now. And you know what you have to do."

"Cancel her bank card for one."

49

"Revoke her privilege to her account."

"I can't do that until tomorrow. First thing when the banks open."

"You need to break it off."

He sighs and rubs his head. "I know." He pushes off the wall and slowly walks off in the direction that Penelope slinked off in. His shoulders slump and he puts his hands in the pockets of his jeans. He stops before he turns the corner and looks back at me. "You, uh… think maybe you could come with me? Keep me from chickening out?"

I push off the wall and follow him with a nod. I hate seeing anyone I'm close to in any kind of pain, but emotional pain is probably the worst. Injuries heal, but the heart? It takes a lot longer. It may never heal completely. The scars left on a heart are permanent. They can change a person for the better, or they can destroy them.

Nick and I find Penelope sitting in the garden in the backyard. She's texting someone and immediately puts her phone away as soon as she sees Nick. I stay back, but within earshot in case my brother needs me. I catch a glimpse of Jason out of the corner of my eye. He walks up next to me as I lean against the house.

"Please tell me this is what I think it is."

"He's about to break up with her. He finally saw her for her true colors. I hope it wasn't too late."

"Did he take her off the accounts?"

"First thing in the morning."

"About damn time. Why does he look so devastated?"

I sigh. "Because when it comes to matters of the heart, it's always harder, Jason."

Penelope storms inside as Nick watches and trudges behind her. She glares at me and Jason on the way by. "You'll pay for this. You all will."

"Looking forward to it, sweetheart." I smirk. She vibrates with anger and storms away. We all listen for the front door to slam before we walk inside.

"She said she's going to ruin me," Nick says.

Jason shrugs. "Let her try."

I give his shoulder a squeeze. "We all have your back."

He nods as he walks up the stairs. Jason and I share a look before we watch Nick climb the last few of them and disappear.

Jason sighs. "You think he'll be okay?"

"Eventually." I pat Jason on the back. "Give him time to come out of it." I give him a soft smile and turn to the kitchen. Few things bring Nick back to himself. Missions are one. Junk food is the other. Given the amount of time we all spend in the gym, we typically don't need to worry about what we eat.

Nachos. Spicy. That's what my brother needs right now. Time with people who care about him. Love him.

He needs his family.

In the end, it's the family that will get him through. Family has always been the one thing we've always been able to count on.

That's something that will never change.

Chapter Eight

✗ Jason ✗

Fucking strobe lights could give a man an aneurysm. I take another drink of my imported beer and glare at the bottle as I peel off the label. Being a twenty-year-old son of a mafia legend takes its toll on a man. I don't mind the perks, but it's hard to live with them.

Morals versus responsibility. It's always been my biggest challenge. I know I've gotten where I am based on my family's illegal activity. My trust fund is dirty money in my eyes. I'm investing dirty money in order to start a business that I want to be legal. Something I want to be successful at. Something for me to make my own way. Something away from the mafia.

The irony isn't lost on me. Starting a legal company with illegal money is one of the most ironic things I can think of, but I need to do it. I'm not like Nick and Ryan or my father. I never have been no matter how much my father tried to make me be.

"You look like someone deep in thought," a soft voice says next to me.

I glance over and give her a soft smile. "Hey, Kelly."

"Penny for your thoughts?" She makes herself comfortable as a guy I've never met drops his hand on her back.

"Hey, gorgeous. Buy you a drink?" he slurs. Dude has definitely had one too many.

"Uh... no." Kelly pushes his hand away, but he doesn't take the hint. His hand instead moves to her leg. She's wearing a short skirt. I watch as he brushes his fingertips up her leg. She slaps his hand away.

"Oh, come on now, honey. Let me buy you a drink." He leans forward and drops his hand on her leg again. She backs into me and tries to shove him off, but he moves in closer and grabs her pussy.

In a flash, I'm on my feet. She screams and pushes him away, but his hold on her is tight. I reach between her legs and grab his wrist. I bend it back and shove him off as she scrambles behind me and falls to her knees.

"She said no. Did you not hear her?" I growl as I force him to his knees.

"I thought she was playing hard to get! Let go, man! Please!"

I look back at Kelly. "Want me to call the police or let him go?"

She shivers and bites her lip. "I..."

I nod and twist his wrist. I feel it snap, and he howls in pain. "If you touch her or another woman without their consent again, I will come after you. Understand me?"

"Yes! Yes! Oh, God. Let me go!"

I let go of his wrist and stand, noticing the crowd of people we've managed to attract. I shoot everyone a dangerous as fuck look. They all go back to doing whatever it was they were doing as the drunk asshole scurries away. I kneel next to Kelly, still curled in a ball on the floor with her knees to her chest.

"You okay?"

Her eyes are filled with unshed tears, but she nods anyway. "Thank you. For helping me."

"You're welcome. What do you say we get you out of here? I can take you home or call you an Uber."

Fear crosses her face. She vigorously shakes her head. "Please don't do that. I...," she trails off and looks at her hands.

I push a strand of hair behind her ear, leaving my hand lingering on her cheek. "Hey. Kel, if you feel safer with me, I'll take you home myself."

She nods and swallows. "Please…" Her voice is barely audible, and she doesn't look back up at me.

"Mr. Crane, the bouncer has taken care of the guy. We've banned him. He won't be back," the bartender says to me.

"Thanks. Get me a bottle of water for her."

"Yes, sir."

I help her to her feet. She clings to me. The bartender hands me the water, and I lead her out to my car. I help her inside. She sips on her water and keeps her eyes straight ahead. I close her door and get into the driver's side.

"Where to?"

She glances at me. "Did you know that wasn't the first time that's happened? Guys are so disgusting when they're drunk. It's so weird. It's shocking at first, but I'm totally desensitized to it. I've had my ass, and my tits grabbed so many times. After the initial shock of it wears off, I'm just… numb."

I shake my head. "He didn't grab your ass or your tits. He grabbed your pussy. No guy should ever think it's okay to grab a woman's ass or tits. Certainly not her pussy. He assaulted you, Kel. Don't ever fucking become desensitized to that."

She nods and goes back to sipping her water. I pull out of the parking lot. "I don't want to go home, Jason. No one's there. I don't want to be alone tonight. I was feeling a little down. It's why I came out in the first place"

"Okay. Where do you want to go?"

"Anywhere. Nowhere."

I glance at her and decide to drive. No destination in mind. Over the past couple of years, Kelly and I have become really good friends. I don't have many of those. I don't let myself get close to anyone but family. It's one of the things I have in common with Ryan. We don't trust anyone easily. Kelly has always been different. Ever since I first confided in her, she's become one of the few people I know I can always count on.

After a long silent drive, I pull off at a lookout point where the entire city lays at our feet. No one ever comes here except me and Ryan.

54

It's part of a piece of property my family owns. About a mile from here is a safehouse deeply hidden in the woods.

We both get out of the car and lean against the hood, quietly watching the twinkling city lights. She leans her head on my shoulder. After a few minutes, she lets out a long breath as she crosses her arms over her chest and rubs them. I put an arm around her and pull her close to my side.

"Cold?"

She shrugs. "A little."

I move her in front of me so her back is to me and wrap my arms around her. I rest my chin on the top of her head. "I should've stepped in sooner."

"I had him handled."

"He grabbed you, Kelly. He wouldn't have if I'd stepped in sooner."

She turns in my arms and encircles her arms around my shoulders, pressing herself against me. With no warning, she stands on her tiptoes, pulls me down to her, and kisses me long and hard. Keeping my arms tightly around her waist, I pull her a little closer and kiss her just as deeply back.

Out of breath after the passionate kiss, we pull away and stare at each other. I've never been shy around women, but I don't know what to say. I sense she needs this, whatever this is, and I don't have the heart to stop her.

Unfortunately, morals get in the way. "Kel, you don't want this. Not with me. You know I won't commit to you. You deserve better than me. We're far better friends."

She smiles sadly and pulls away. She leans against the hood of my black Corvette and bites her lip. "You're probably right." She crosses her arms over her chest again and rubs her arms. She crosses her legs and sighs heavily.

"Fuck it." I turn and lean her back against the hood of my car, surprising her. She gasps when my lips crash to hers, but she eagerly returns it. Her nails dig into my arms when I crawl on top of her, tugging her further up the hood of the car so she's more against the windshield and her legs aren't dangling off the bumper.

"Mmm…," she moans.

I kiss down her jaw to her neck. "Are you sure this is what you want? I don't want to ruin what we have."

"Why can't it be a friends with benefits thing? It's not like you've never touched me before."

I smile as I reach between her legs. She's not wrong. We major in the same thing. We have a lot of the same classes. There have been several days where we've both been incredibly frustrated over one thing or another. In the back of the sometimes dark, and sometimes not dark, classroom, we've both gotten each other off. If we weren't watching a movie or a PowerPoint or something and the lights were on, we'd hide ourselves from other people's view with jackets or sweaters. Lucky for us, no one sat near us. The entire back row was free of others in several of our classes. A perk to being a business major is large classrooms and less students.

I lick across her neck and throat to her shoulder and collarbone, kissing to her chest as I slide her panties aside and thrust two fingers into her already wet and wanting center. Her nails dig into my shoulders. She throws her head back and arches into my hand. I've learned she loves hard and deep thrusts. If I do it fast while running my thumb over her clit, she comes almost immediately.

I do just that. She thrusts her hips against my hand in time with my pace and latches onto my cock with her hand. She squeezes and rubs. My eyes nearly roll back into my head as I nip at her nipple.

I moan and flick her clit. "Oh, fuck…"

She unbuttons my button and unzips my zipper with one hand. She pulls my cock out of my pants, stroking fast as she twists her wrist. She starts quivering. Her thighs tremble. Her pussy tightens around my fingers, and she comes with a scream.

"Jason! Oh!" She shakes and pulses around my fingers while she strokes me.

"Jesus, Kel." I slowly pull my fingers out of her and reach into my pocket to pull out my wallet. I pull out a condom and tear it open with my teeth. She watches in complete fascination while I roll it with one hand over my length. I position myself at her entrance, pushing her panties aside again. "Is this what you want?" My tip is just against her, but I don't enter her. After what she's been through, I want to be sure this is really what she wants from me. What she needs right now.

56

"Yes. Please." She puts both hands on my face and pulls me down to kiss her. I slowly slide inside her inch by inch.

"Oh, God…," I whisper into her mouth. She's tight as hell, and I'm a little afraid I'm going to tear her pussy apart given how big I am compared to her.

She grips my shoulders and squeezes her eyes shut as she relaxes into me. "I've never… had… someone so big," she gasps.

I give her time to adjust to me as I watch her. After a few moments she slowly opens her eyes and looks up at me. I push her hair out of her face. "You ready?"

She nods. I start slowly thrusting, pulling all the way out and pushing all the way back in, letting her get used to me. She arches into me, tugging at my hair and moaning as she starts meeting my thrusts. She wraps her legs around me.

I slide in deeper. "Ah… God." I tangle her hair around my fist and thrust faster as she meets every one of them, giving just as well as she's receiving. Before long, we're battling for control. Her nails dig into my back while mine squeeze her tits. We slide against each other faster and faster until I'm slamming into her with all I'm worth. The car underneath us rocks back and forth. We're tugging at each other's clothes and hair.

"Jason! Yes! Yes… Yes!"

"Fuck, Kel!"

Our bodies slam together against the hood of the car with the city lights below us, and dark as midnight sky above us. Her thighs quake as my stomach clenches. She tightens and starts pulsing hard around me as I thrust deep and hard inside her.

"Ah! Jason!" She pulls my hair as she comes.

"Kelly!" Our voices reverberate through the quiet air. A jolt travels through my spine. She rips my orgasm from me as I slam into her one last time and come deep within her warm, wet walls. We both collapse against the hood of the car, breathing hard and trying to catch our breath.

"Oh, God, Jason."

I smile into her hair and slowly pull out of her after a few moments. I stand and pull the condom off while she sits on the hood of my car straightening her panties and clothing. I open the driver's side door and reach in for a tissue. I wrap the condom up and clean myself off as I hand her a couple to do the same. She takes them gratefully and wipes her thighs.

"You know this was a one time thing."

"I know, Jason."

"We can't do this again."

"You don't do relationships. I understand. I knew what I was getting into. I'm a big girl. I needed that, and judging from what just happened, I think you needed it just as badly. What's wrong?"

I pack myself away as I sigh. She stays on the hood of my car and looks up at me. "I have a lot on my mind."

"Your business you want to start and starting it with money that isn't clean?"

"That, but I think what's bothering me the most is Nick. I'm worried about him. He broke up with fucking Penelope today."

"Isn't that a good thing?"

"It's a great thing. The problem is he seemed pretty upset about it. He discovered her true intentions."

She jumps off the car and hugs me. For some reason, the comfort makes me feel better. I breathe a sigh of relief and feel her smile against my chest. "With you, Ryan, and your family by his side, Nick is going to be just fine. I promise."

I squeeze her a little tighter, but I know she's right. Our family bond is strong, but the bond between the three of us brothers is impenetrable.

Chapter Nine

⚔ Nick ⚔

I groan at the shrill sound of my alarm clock going off. If I didn't need to get up, I'd probably throw the damn thing out the window.

But I can't.

I need to call the bank and get that fucking gold-digging bitch off my accounts before she screws me over. I can't believe I let it go on this far.

I push myself up as someone knocks on my door. I rub my eyes and walk to it, opening it slowly. "What?" I ask as my eyes focus on my brothers.

Ryan pushes by me, and Jason follows, giving me an apologetic look. "Sorry. Ryan said you needed moral support."

"Yeah, sure. Whatever," I grumble. We all sit on my bed, and I have to laugh. None of us have bothered to get dressed. We're all sitting here in boxers and nothing else.

"What the fuck are you laughing at?" Ryan growls.

"Look at us." I gesture between the three of us. Before long we're all laughing.

"I guess some things are more important than clothes," Jason says as I start dialing the bank's number. We all quiet down as I put it on speaker, and it starts ringing.

"Bank of New York Mellon. How may I help you?"

"Hey, my name is Nickolas Crane. Can I speak with my private banker, please? Mr. Mort."

"Sure thing, Mr. Crane. Let me place you on a brief hold and transfer you right away."

"Thank you."

"Hopefully Penelo-slut wasn't standing outside the damn bank door this morning to clean you out after you canceled her cards," Ryan mumbles.

"I still don't know if she's capable of that," I say, shaking my head. "But after last night, I don't know what she's capable of anymore."

Jason raises an eyebrow. "You mean before she left, or did something else happen?"

"Give me your phone," I say, holding out my hand. Ryan hands over his phone, and I quickly pull up Blaze Edge Magazine. I hand it back to him, and Jason leans over and looks at the headline.

"Holy shit," Ryan whispers. The headline and story are all about how I beat her up and left her for dead. The images are of her bruised and battered, but anyone looking closely can see it's all makeup.

"Mr. Crane. How may I assist you today?"

"Mr. Mort, I need to get my ex off my accounts immediately."

"Sure. I'll just need you to come in and take care of some paperwork for me. I'll need your signature -"

"Mr. Mort, it's Ryan Crane. This is time-sensitive. Can you fax the paperwork? He'll sign it right away and fax it back."

Mr. Mort clears his throat. "Mr. Crane, I understand, but federal regulations and bank policy require a signature. It can't be a photocopy."

"It's not a photocopy. It's a fax," I say incredulously.

"Unfortunately, for us, it wouldn't be. We need the original. I can have all of the paperwork ready for you, but you'll have to come in and sign in person."

I look at Ryan and swallow hard. I can feel myself starting to panic. He grabs my phone, eyes flashing fury. "Mr. Mort, I understand, but this is an emergency. There must be something you can do. Can you suspend all of his accounts?"

"Not unless there's fraudulent activity. Otherwise, I still need a signature from Mr. Crane saying he wants his accounts suspended for a particular period of time."

Ryan shakes his head. "So, what you're telling me is if Nick were out of the country and found out his fiancé were going to clean out his accounts in retaliation for breaking up with her, you couldn't do anything for him."

"Mr. Crane, my hands are tied. She has access to his accounts. They both signed paperwork, and I need signed paperwork by him. We'll have to close his accounts and open new ones because without her signature we can't remove her from the joint accounts."

Ryan grits his teeth as hard as he grips my phone. "Mr. Mort, you better pray nothing happens to any of his accounts before we get there." Ryan hangs up. "Get dressed. Quickly."

It takes minutes before we're all downstairs and getting ready to fly out the door. I find my heart is racing, and I'm starting to get a headache. Worst headache I've ever had.

"Where are you three off to so early? Neither of you have class until this afternoon," mom says from the hallway.

"We're closing out Nick's accounts before Penelo-slut can fuck them up," Ryan says as he leads us out the door. She stares after us, slightly confused.

"I'll explain later." I smile softly at her as I close the door behind us. We all jump in one of the guard's SUV's. It's the only vehicle big enough to fit three people. The three of us drive sports cars that don't have backseats.

Ryan speeds through the streets, getting to the bank in record time. He parks in a VIP space I'm sure he shouldn't be in, but Ryan believes the world revolves around him. Parking VIP is nothing new.

"If you get another vehicle towed, dad's head may actually explode," Jason chuckles.

"He needs some excitement in his life," Ryan laughs as we walk into the bank. Ryan leads us up to a teller and moves aside for me.

"Good morning," the friendly young teller says. I give her my sexiest smile. "I need to speak with Mr. Mort right away."

"Sure," she smiles back. "Let me see if he's available." She taps a few keys. I get a stabbing pain in my head, but fight it off, continuing to watch her. "It looks like he's in a meeting, but if you sit down right over there, I'll tell him you're here." She smiles up at points to an area with a few chairs and a coffee pot.

I look back at her. "Can you send him a message now, please? It's important."

She bites her lip, and I can see the moment she melts under my intense gaze. "I'm really not supposed to interrupt," she says quietly.

I smile a little cockily. I'm fully aware I'm attractive. I don't use that to my advantage as often as Jason and Ryan, but I do it when I need to. "It would mean a lot to me…" I look at her name tag and let my eyes linger on her cleavage a moment longer than necessary. I look back up at her, and she visibly shivers. "Chelsea."

She smiles and taps a few keys. She waits a moment and looks back up at me. "He said he'll be down in a moment."

"Thank you, honey," I drawl as I wink. The three of us walk over to the waiting area and sit.

Jason looks at his watch. "I really don't like this."

"Me either, Jas," Ryan says as he leans back. We're all tense. I rub my temple as we wait.

"Mr. Crane," Mr. Mort says quietly. I look up at him. He's sweating and loosening his tie. He motions for us all to follow him. I exchange a nervous look with Jason and Ryan as we follow. He closes us into an office and turns to us. "I was just on the phone with the bank president discussing your situation. I got an okay to put a hold on your accounts, but when I pulled them up, they were all empty."

"What?" I slump against the wall and sink to the floor.

"There was a large cash withdrawal and a transfer this morning just as we opened. I was not notified. The teller who made the transaction has been fired because that type of withdrawal needs to be okayed. It wasn't."

Ryan glances down at me as Jason kneels at my side. "What was the teller's name?"

Mr. Mort looks at him, terrified. "I… am not allowed to… give that information to you." He sits on the edge of the desk. Ryan steps forward, crowding him. He reaches up and loosens his tie more than it had been. He's clearly nervous. For the hundredth time in my life, I'm glad Ryan is on my side.

"Who…" Ryan leans down with both hands on the desk. Mr. Mort swallows hard. "Was… the… teller?"

"A-Abernathy K-Koontz."

Ryan stands up and reaches a hand down to help me up. I take his hand, and he pulls me up effortlessly. "You okay?"

"I…" I shake my head, unsure how to answer. "I don't know."

"You'll be okay," he assures me. I glance back at Mr. Mort, who's hyperventilating on the floor, as Jason and I follow Ryan out. We don't say a word until we get to the SUV and pile in. Ryan steps on the gas and peels out. He races through the streets towards home. I watch the city blur as we drive, unsure how Ryan never gets caught by the police with the way he speeds through New York as he does.

"How did this happen?" I wonder. "How could she do this?"

"It's what she's wanted from the beginning," Jason answers.

"I was just too stupid to let myself believe it," I growl getting angrier and angrier with myself. Ryan pulls into the driveway. We all get out. I'm both dazed and pissed off. I look around, suddenly in the living room. "How the fuck did I get here?"

Ryan and Jason look at each other, then back at me. Ryan sits me down and looks at Jason. "Stay with him."

"Got it." Jason sits next to me as Ryan jogs out of the room. "You don't look so good."

I rub my temple again and lean back against the couch as nausea overwhelms me. "I started getting a headache this morning. It's turned into a full-blown migraine. I really need to lay down." Jason stands and helps me lay down, putting a pillow underneath my head. I close my eyes, and the world fades away in seconds.

XXX

I groan and cough as I open my eyes. I blink a few times and feel someone sit next to me. A cold washcloth is put on my forehead. I jerk slightly.

"It's okay, honey. It's just me," mom says softly as she wipes away sweat from my forehead and face. "How do you feel?"

I try to sit up, but she gently pushes me back down. There's no use fighting her. "Better. How long have I been out?"

"Most of the day."

"What? Mom, I need to get up. I have to figure out what the fuck that bitch did with my accounts."

"Your brothers and father dealt with that already."

I look up at her. "And?"

"And… they traced your money to an offshore account in the Cayman Islands. I don't understand it all, but the teller at our bank transferred it to some private account. From there, it was transferred several more times. It was withdrawn from the bank in the Cayman Islands. They had the security cameras pulled. It was Penelope. We have no way of tracking it further, and she disappeared."

I swipe my hands over my face. "I don't care about the money. I don't care that she made a fool out of me. All I care about is what my family thinks of me. I fucked up."

"Oh, honey." Mom leans down and hugs me. "That's not something you need to worry about."

"You all told me to steer clear of her. I should've listened. Now, I'm left with nothing. I don't even feel heartbroken. I feel empty and disappointed in myself. Angry." I bury my face in mom's hair as she squeezes me tightly. I clench my jaw and shut my eyes to keep the tears threatening to fall from doing just that. "Angry because you all put trust in me and gave me all of this stuff and opportunities in life that I'd never have had otherwise. I fucked up. I fucked all of that up."

"Nick. You know that you could never be a disappointment to us. She obviously had an elaborate plan she's been working on for a long time. The guy at the bank? The teller? She was working with him. The transfer that was made at the bank here was a woman they hired to pretend to be her. The signature didn't match. He used some of the money to jump on a plane while the rest was transferred. The plane stopped in Orlando, and from there, he vanished just like she did. The woman they hired pretending to be her has vanished as well. This isn't your fault, sweetheart."

"It's a lesson to never trust anyone but family again."

64

"Nickolas. You can't give up on love. Ever. When the right woman comes along, you'll know. Until then, you'll be careful."

I loosen my grip on her, and she pulls away. She puts her hand on my chest, and I rest mine on top of hers. "Listen to my family. My instincts. Never ignore either."

She smiles softly. "That would be helpful." She cups my cheek. "We replaced the money in your trust fund."

"What? Mom, you -"

"Nickolas. There's no arguing. This wasn't your fault. You shouldn't be punished for someone else's actions."

"But had I listened, it wouldn't have happened."

"Sweetheart, it doesn't matter. It's been done. You're our son. Just as Ryan and Jason are. We'd have done the exact same thing for them. That's the end of the story. There will be no more argument."

I know arguing is pointless, so I stop. Instead, I work on fighting back the tears that threaten to fall from my eyes. Sometimes, the love this family shows is overwhelming at best. I don't know what I did to deserve a family like this. I don't know what I did to deserve the bond we share.

I look up and sit up slowly as my brothers and father walk into the room. They all surround me and hug me, saying how much they love me, and the dam breaks. I rarely cry, but there's no way I can hold back now.

They all stay gathered around me and hug me as I sob. Tears of joy or heartbreak, I don't know. All I know is they're all I need.

Chapter Ten

☒ Ryan ☒

(One Week Later)

I stare at my dad, astonished. "You're telling me that this Lucinio Mafia is still a fucking problem?"

"Even bigger than we thought," dad confirms.

I sink into my chair. "You said they were taken care of. That we wouldn't have to worry about them anymore."

"That was before they decided it would be fun to mess with your mother."

My mouth drops open, my fists automatically clench, and, though I can't see it, I feel my coffee-colored eyes darken to black. I clench my teeth together. "What... happened?"

"She was shopping. She was approached by a male she hadn't seen before. She had a guard with her, but he had gone to the bathroom. The male dragged her out to an alley near the store. She was shoved against the wall of the building. Other males showed up." Dad pauses to control his rising temper. I watch as his neck reddens. He grips the desk as hard as I'm gripping the chair.

"If they touched her…," I growl darkly. Dangerously.

"They roughed her up. Hit her a couple times. They sent her away with a message for us."

I glare. "What was the message?"

"That if we didn't back out of L.A., they'd come after everyone we love and care about. She was first. It was a warning. They said next time she won't be so lucky."

I stand and pace. "There won't be a fucking next time."

"That's not all. Sit down, Ryan."

"No. If I sit down, I'm going to rip a hole in the chair."

He nods. "We found evidence of… a…" My dad swallows and shakes his head as he himself stands and paces. I watch him. He kicks the wall, and then leans his head against it. "A child sex trade ring."

I stop pacing. "A… what?"

"Yeah." He pushes off the wall and paces his office. "Right under our noses. In our territory. It looks like it's us running it."

I sink to the floor and sit. "We'd never do that."

"We know that. The police don't. They're after us."

I shake my head. "No. No. I have a friend who's the daughter of the Commissioner. She'll help clear us."

Dad looks down at me. "You think so?"

I stand and take out my phone. "Mia knows me. Us. She knows we'd never do that shit." I dial her number and pace the office as dad watches me.

"Hey, Ry. Miss me?"

I can't help but smile. "Immensely. I need your help."

"Sure. What's up?"

I love how she doesn't question me. She's ready and willing to help. "There's another mafia we're dealing with. As big as us but far more… uh… ruthless, I guess. Dangerous. They're running a child sex trade ring."

"That's… disgusting."

"They're making it look like it's us."

"No way. Even I know your family wouldn't do that."

"You may trust us, but the NYPD doesn't."

"You want me to talk to my dad."

I rub my forehead as I stop pacing. "Is that too much to ask?"

"Ryan, my dad already knows. And he doesn't believe it's you."

My eyes shoot to my father's. "What?"

"I've heard all about it. He was talking to my mom about something you guys did, and how frustrating it was that he couldn't catch you and prove it. Then he started talking about this underground child sex trade ring. How on the outside it looked like you, but he knew better. He said it wasn't your style."

"Thank God for that. It isn't. Think he can get everyone else to see that?"

"He's working on it, Ry. He said it would work out a lot better for him if he could get you guys to put your talent for criminal activity on the right side of the law and help him stop it instead of giving him more to do by adding to it."

I chuckle softly. "One day."

"I know. You can't take over fast enough. Look. Just know he's working on it. If you could get him evidence somehow..."

"How, sweetheart?"

"I don't know. Anonymously? It would help."

I sit down in the chair and glance at my dad. He's watching me curiously. "I'll think of something."

"I know you will. Get it to me. I'll give it to him."

"You can't tell him where you got it, or he won't be able to use it."

"I know. I'll keep you out of it. But if you want my help, and his, you need to be on the right side of the law. Sort of. You know what I mean."

"I need to help the cops. Got it."

"Not like it would be an issue for you. It's what you want anyway, right?"

"What I want and what the boss wants are very different things."

She laughs quietly. "I know. Get me something. And come over later. My roommate is gone for the weekend, and I'm bored."

I smile. "You're the only girl I've been with more than once."

"I must be really good, then," she jokes. She uses me just as much as I use her, and we both know it.

"No comment. I can't come over later. We need to deal with this, and I need to get you that evidence."

She sighs dramatically, and I laugh. "Fine. I guess I'll use my trusty vibrator tonight."

I groan. "Stop it. I'll call you when I have it."

She laughs. "I'll be waiting."

I shake my head and hang up as I look back at dad. "She said her dad knows it isn't us. It's not our style. But we need to get him evidence. I can bring it to Mia. She'll get it to him."

"You trust this girl?"

"She's more than a notch on my bedpost, if that's what you're asking. We have fun, but she's a good friend. Yeah. I trust her."

He nods. "I trust your instincts. Get ready to go. We're going to get her that evidence. I won't have some lowlife amoeba making it look like we're doing something as sick as a sex trade ring of any kind. Let alone one involving children."

XXX

Hours later, when the sun is rising, dad and I trudge into the house. I fall down onto the couch. "That was fucking exhausting. I don't remember when the last time I slept was."

Dad sits next to me. "It's been a while since I pulled an all-nighter like that."

"This week has been fucked up. First Penelope. Now this?"

"At least we have that evidence. Get that to Mia. We don't need every law enforcement division after us. We have enough to deal with."

"It wouldn't be that way if you'd listen to me. Go legit."

"We've talked about this. This isn't the time to hash it over again. I'm far too tired."

My phone rings as dad is standing. I don't recognize the number, but decide to answer it anyway. "Hello?"

"Is this Ryan Crane?" The voice is frantic, and I raise an eyebrow. I place my hand on dad's arm as I turn the phone on speaker.

"Yeah. Who's this?" I look up as Charlie walks into the room. Dad puts a hand up to silence him as he begins talking.

"This is Nelson Tate. I'm a Police Commissioner with the NYPD. I… Please, I need your help." His voice cracks.

"You're Mia's father," I say.

"Yes! She's been kidnapped!" He speaks rapidly. I can barely make out the words. "She got me a message that said to contact you. You could help. Please. Please help me find my daughter. She's gone! Missing! I -"

"Commissioner Tate. Stop. Slow down. Tell me what happened."

He takes a deep, shaky breath. "I got a text message from her at two in the morning. All it said was help. I texted her and called her. She didn't answer. I've been searching. Tracking her phone. I know she's in L.A., but I have nothing more. She managed to send a message to me five minutes ago. She said to contact you. You'll help. Please. Please find my daughter."

"Fuck. Okay. Tell me where you last pinpointed her." My dad and Charlie are already in motion. I know they're going to wake my brothers.

"We had her in L.A. It looks like somewhere in the Palisade Hills area. After I got that last message, her signal disappeared."

"They may have shut her phone off. Or she sensed danger and did it herself. Your daughter is a smart girl, Commissioner."

"I'm at the airport waiting on standby for a flight to L.A." He chokes back what sounds to be a strangled sob. "Please help me. If she trusts you, I know I can. My daughter has a good head on her shoulders. Good instincts."

"I agree. She's a good girl. A good friend."

"I'll do whatever you want. Please help me find her."

"You don't need to do anything for me. Mia is a good friend. We're already mobilizing. We'll meet you at JFK in twenty minutes."

"You'll never get through security in twenty minutes!" he says confused.

"Go to gate A. Tell them you're with Ryan Crane. By the time you get there, they'll have orders to board you on my jet."

He lets out a shaky breath. "Okay."

"Twenty minutes. We'll be there." I hang up as my brothers come down the stairs with dad.

Mom follows. She walks directly to me and hugs me. "Be careful."

I hug her back tightly. "We will."

She pulls away, and Jason hands me a duffle bag. "Your gear. Let's get out of here. End this fucking thing once and for all."

70

"Chopper's parked on the roof. Jas, I need you to fly. I have orders to give and calls to make."

We all head to the roof as I take out my phone. I bark out orders to my flight staff and call in my flight plan. Jason flies us to the airport while I mobilize a team in L.A. By the time we get to JFK and land, my jet is gassed up on the tarmac and ready to go.

"What do we do with the chopper?" Nick asks.

"I'll take care of it," one of the people from the airport says behind us.

I nod as the staff grabs our gear and brings it to the jet. "Commissioner Tate on board?"

"Yes, sir," the staff member says.

"Captain ready to go?" I ask.

"He's doing his pre-flight check. He said five minutes."

"Good. Thank you." I jog up the stairs. Jason, Nick, my dad, and several guards are already on board and strapping in. Commissioner Tate watches everyone from a seat in the back corner of the plane. I make my way to him and offer a hand. "Commissioner. I'm Ryan Crane."

He hesitantly stands and shakes my hand, keeping an eye on all of the activity as everyone settles. "Mr. Crane this is all…"

"I know." I let go of his hand. "Overwhelming. I get it, but I'm not the bad guy here."

"This time anyway."

I give him a tired smile and nod. "Yeah. This time. Look. I like Mia. My relationship with her means a lot to me." I gesture to my family. "My brothers and my dad will do whatever it takes to help. I know you and I are on different sides of the line here, but Mia is important to me. You may not trust me or my family, but you can trust that I'll save her. I'll do whatever it takes to find your daughter."

"I already said if she trusts you then I do." He looks up at me as he sits down. "I'll do whatever needs to be done to find my daughter and bring her home safe. I hope we aren't too late."

I sit next to him and begin explaining what's going to happen when we get to L.A. as the plane takes off. When we're in the air, we all gather and formulate a plan of attack.

By the time we land, we all know our roles and what needs to be done. We have no time to do any surveillance ourselves and will need to

71

rely on what I've sent our team in L.A. to do. I hope it's enough, but that little voice in the back of my head keeps telling me that we're too late.

✕✕✕

"I don't know how you're going to do this," Jason says as I yawn. "You haven't slept."

"Simple," I say. "I'm going to sleep right now. We're going to trust our team to do what they need to do."

"That's blind trust if I've ever heard it."

"Jas, we have no choice." I lay back on the bed and close my eyes. "It's no different than any other mission. We rely on our team to get us intel. We're relying on them just as much now. Maybe more." I open one eye. "Go to sleep. You need to be ready. We all do."

"How big is this mafia, Ryan? I need to know."

I sigh and open both eyes. "They're big, Jas. But we aren't going into this blind. We have our surveillance team out there right now gathering intel. By the time we get there tonight, we'll have more than enough information to go in and make intelligent decisions."

"I'm scared, Ry. I'm always a little nervous going into missions. I've never been able to be calm and cool and collected like you and Nick, but I've never been scared. I'm terrified going into this. I've got so many bad feelings about this that my bad feelings have bad feelings."

"We go in like we always do. We stick to the plan. We rely on each other. We rely on our team. That's what we do." I close my eyes again. "We need to sleep, Jason." I feel him lay on the bed next to me and glance at him, but say nothing.

Ever since Jason was a kid, whenever he's feared something, he's climbed in my bed. Obviously the older we've gotten, the less he's done that. He hasn't in many, many years. Probably since he was twelve and had a nightmare we all were killed in an explosion.

I can tell how scared he is right now, though. It's not like when we were kids, but I've always been Jason's calming force. No one, not even our parents, has been able to calm him like me. Most of the time, just my presence is enough to ease his nerves and fears.

He curls up on his side, and I know he's watching the door. I sigh and sit up. "Switch me sides, Jas."

He glances at me before he sits up and moves to the other side of the bed. "Thanks."

I lay down with my back to Jason, facing the door. It doesn't take long before my brother's breathing evens out. I glance over my shoulder and see he's sleeping peacefully. I know he's calmer. No matter the dangers we may face tonight, I'm happy to be the person that eases his mind now.

XXX

I lay prone in the dirt hidden by brush and the dark as fuck night. You'd think with all the lights and traffic in L.A., there wouldn't be a chance in hell of it being this dark. But here we are. Shielded from unwanted attention by the midnight sky.

I've never had an issue with darkness. Even as a child, darkness was never a fear. I've never been afraid of anything except losing someone I love.

Before every single mission I've ever been on, I've always done one thing. I've always made sure my loved ones know that I love them. After every mission I make sure everyone is accounted for. If one of my brother's isn't with me or father, I call them. I call my mother to check in. But the one thing I've always done before is close my eyes and run my fingers across the worn, leather band tied around my wrist.

It was given to me long ago by my grandfather. He said it always brought him the confidence he needed to go into battle and come out alive. It seemed to work for him because he died peacefully in his sleep a few years ago. He had heart complications. One night it stopped beating, but he felt no pain. He died with a smile on his face.

"Ready to go, Cobra two?" my dad's deep voice says into my earpiece.

I clear my mind and focus. I know there are six guards inside. I know Matthew Lucinio is inside with his wife and two sons. I know there are guards outside, and I know how many. I know my team is ready to strike given the command. I know where the fucker is keeping Mia.

Jason lies prone next to me. Nick is with dad. I look at Jason. He nods. "Cobra two ready," I say.

73

"Everyone move in. Take your targets on the way. Go," dad commands. We all move with calculated precision to the dark and still house. Jason and I slide silently along the back of the house until we reach the stairs leading to the basement. We stealthily walk down them until we get to the door. Our mission is Mia.

"I really don't like this, Ry. Something isn't right."

"I feel it, Jas, but we need to trust our team." I quietly jimmy the door open. Jason and I slip inside, keeping our eyes peeled for any danger in the dark. Right where our surveillance said she would be, I find Mia in the middle of the room tied to a chair and completely naked.

"Jesus. What the fuck did they do to her?"

"Don't ask questions now. We need to get her out of here. Cover me."

"Ryan?" she moans weakly.

"Yeah, Mia. It's me. We got you."

"They…" She starts to cry as I unlock the handcuffs around her wrist.

"I know, baby. Let us get you out of here. Don't talk." I pull her up. She collapses. I catch her and lift her into my arms. "Cobra two and Cobra three have the princess."

"Get her to safety," someone I don't recognize says in my ear.

I pause on my way to the door and meet Jason's eyes. "Who the fuck said that? That wasn't dad."

Jason immediately closes the door and raises his weapon, doing a sweep of the basement. "We need a way out."

Mia tightens her arms around my neck. "Wh-what's h-happening?"

"Get us out of here, Jason," I say.

"Ryan, don't come into the house! They have us surrounded! Get out!" dad yells into the earpiece.

Jason and I immediately take out our earpieces and stomp on them. Someone knows we're here and figured out a way to hack into our communication signal. They know every single move we say we're making with our communication.

"Ryan, what do we do?" Jason asks, panicking.

"First, we don't panic." I slowly let Mia down and take off my bulletproof vest. I quickly take off my black long sleeve shirt and give it to her. "Put that on." She takes it shakily, choking back sobs. I put my hands

74

on both of her shoulders. "Mia, honey. Look at me." She grips my arms and does as she's told. "You trust me, right?"

"Y-yes. Yes. I trust you."

I help her put the shirt on. "Then you need to trust me when I tell you that I'm going to get us out of this. I need to save my family. I need you to be strong for me. Can you do that?" I put my vest back on over my black t-shirt.

She nods. "Yes."

I quickly take the Glock I keep strapped to my leg and give it to her. "You're dad's a cop. Please tell me you've shot a gun before."

"At… the… range. At targets."

"Anyone but me or Jason or Nick or my father come down here, shoot them. Understand?"

"It's dark! How will I know?" She hesitantly takes the gun.

"Code word," Jason says. "If you don't hear us say racoon, you shoot."

I nod. "Racoon. Got it?"

"Yes," she says as she nods.

"Good. I want you to hide. Go."

"Promise you'll come back for me."

I hug her for a moment, and then lean in and kiss her, mostly to calm us both down. I pull away slowly. "Mia, I won't leave you here. Now go." My eyes have adjusted pretty well to the dark. I see her hide behind a few crates. I ready my rifle and turn to Jason. "We go up. We open the door. I go low. You go high."

"Got it."

I lead us up the stairs. At the top, I take a deep breath. I kick the door open and have no time to react before a hail of gunfire reigns down. Jason and I dive for the ground and scurry for any kind of cover. We crawl around a corner and come face to face with our team.

"I told you to stay down there! What the fuck were you thinking?" dad yells.

"Dad, please! Stop talking!" Nick looks at me. "Fucking Lucinio shot him point blank to the chest!"

Everything seems to go in slow motion. Jason is covering his head and staring in horror at the scene in front of us. Three bodies bleeding on the ground, all good guards. Dad is covered in blood lying on the ground.

Nick is crying, also covered in blood, as he keeps pressure on dad's wound. Our guards are shooting into the other room. Bullets are ricocheting all around.

"Advance!" someone yells. I don't know who, but I shake my head, forcing myself to snap out of it.

I look at Jason and Nick. "Get him out of here!" I point to two of my guards. "You and you. Cover them! Go!" My commanding voice snaps everyone into action. I stand and lead who I have left around the corner. The shooting is deafening, but I need to protect my family. If I can keep everyone in here on me, it'll give them a chance to get away.

When the gunfire settles, I don't know how long of an amount of time later, I'm still standing with hardly any of my team. Bodies lay strewn all over the room from both sides of the battle. I still have a few, but Matthew fucking Lucinio has lost them all.

Except one. One is on his knees looking up at me. My gun is leveled between his eyes. He can't be more than a teenager. It has to be one of the sons.

"What's your name?" I growl.

The kid looks up at me with tears in his eyes. "Alex," he whispers.

For the first time in my life, my finger shakes on the trigger. I don't know why, but something about this kid doesn't seem to hit me right. Killing him feels… like the wrong thing to do. I lower the gun a little. He watches my every move with curiosity and total terror.

"You're one of the sixteen-year-old twins," I say as the intel we gathered on the Lucinio Mafia comes back to me. "You're the one in the line to take over." I glare and raise my gun back to his head.

"Yes! But I don't want it!" He holds his hands up in surrender, and the tears he fought to hold back start falling. "My brother, Josh, wants it. He's better fit for the job! He wants to turn it legit, and our father doesn't want that, so he's trying to force it on me." He looks up at me. "I don't want it. I don't want any of this. You have to believe me."

"Where's your father and brother now?"

"My father fled as soon as you started advancing. He said we couldn't let you take out the leader or we'd fail as a mafia. He said someone had to stay and lead. He made me do it and left me and Josh. I made Josh run. He didn't want to, but I made him. I wanted to run, too, but I couldn't leave my team to fight alone with no direction. I don't know where Josh ran. Let me make sure he's okay. Let me find him. Please. And then I don't care what you do to me as long as he's safe." He looks at me with the sincerest eyes I've ever seen. He's not very good at hiding emotion.

I lower my gun and give him a hand up. "You really don't want this?"

He takes my hand, hesitantly, and I pull him up. "No. I want to go to college and get the fuck out of this life. My father has other plans. He's not afraid to use violence to get it either." He holds out his arms, and I see more scratching and bruising than I've ever seen on anyone. He lifts his shirt, and I hiss at the purplish bruises all over his chest.

"Fuck."

"This beating was for getting in his way of getting to my brother."

"Ryan, we're clear. There's no one else here. We checked every room. The bird got away. We can't find the wife or other son."

I look up as Charlie walks in the room. "Clear out. Gather everyone and leave."

His mouth nearly hits the ground. "But what about getting information out of him?" He nods to Alex.

"You have your orders. Get out. Now."

He nods. "Yes, sir."

I wait until it's just me and Alex left in the room. Alex looks up at me. "He won't go after you again. He barely escaped with his life and lost I don't know how many guards."

"I'll deal with it when he does. And you're going to help me. If you don't want this, you'll help me keep him at bay."

"I planned to take over and hand control over to Josh, but he'd never allow that. He'd kill us both. I don't know how I can help you. I don't have much sway."

"You're going to feed me information. Give me your phone." He hands it over with no questions. I put my phone number in it and send myself a text so I have his. "But above and beyond that, you're going to call me if you need help."

"He's... been making me and Josh go on missions by ourselves. Lead them."

"I'll help you with them. Call. I can help prepare you and your brother for this so when he does give up control, you'll know what you're doing and your brother can take it in the direction he wants to."

"Wait. You want to help me? Even though one of my family's mafia's guards just killed your father?"

I pause. I decide after a few seconds to not correct him and tell him his father did it. Nick had to have seen it. He wouldn't have accused Matthew otherwise. It's not his style. I don't doubt Alex would believe me, but he's been through a lot, and it doesn't matter anyway. Not right now. Right now, the priority is making sure my father is okay, and that we all make it out of here. Alex and his brother included.

"Consider it a quid pro quo. You help me. I'll help you." He watches me. "Look, Alex, I'm not out to get you. You're a kid. You and your brother are trying to do exactly what I plan to do. Which says to me that you aren't a bad guy. Call me. If you need help, or if you need to talk."

"Why not just kill me?"

"Because it would be like killing myself. Or my brother. He's a lot like you. You're a lot like us both. You deserve a chance to prove yourself. I don't have any doubt you will." I look around the house. "Go find your brother. Let me know he's okay. And don't make me regret sparing you tonight. If you cross me, I won't hesitate next time." I don't say another word as I turn away and walk back to the door for the basement. I open it only a crack. "Mia? Racoon."

"Ryan?"

"I'm coming down, honey. It's safe." I open the door further and take another glance back at Alex.

"I won't let you down," he says. I nod as he turns and runs from the room in search of his twin.

"Mia? What do you say we get the fuck out of here?" I say as I get to the bottom stair. She launches herself at me. I lift her off the ground in a tight hug and don't let her go as I walk out of the basement and up the stairs in the back of the house. As soon as we get to the SUV, I let her down. I hand her a blanket I have in an emergency kit in the back. I get information on my father about what hospital he's at and drive towards it using GPS. I've never understood L.A. and have to use GPS every time I come here.

I fly through the streets as fast as I dare, worried about my father and curious about the future and what it will hold. I'm not ready to take over, but I know instinctively I'll need to. I shouldn't have spent so much time being rebellious. I accepted my fate of running the Crane Mafia when I was a child and was first told of my inheritance. I never dreamt it would be so soon, but no one knows what the future will hold.

All we can do for ourselves is prepare for it the best we can.

Chapter Eleven

☒ Jason ☒

(Two Years Later)

"It's pointless. I'm never getting through this," Ryan complains. He groans and puts his head down on the desk in his office in his Manhattan mansion.

"You will because if you don't, you'll never understand the business side of this mafia. You need to understand this."

"I have you. You can deal with this shit."

I shake my head, determined for him to understand the numbers in front of him. "Ryan, it's been two years since you took over. You got through school and got your business degree. You made the mafia legit just like you wanted to. If you want it to be successful, you need to understand the business side of it just like you understand the rest of it. I can't keep doing this for you. I have my own company to run."

He groans again. "I'll hire someone," he says into his arms.

"No. Come on. You need to do this. Now look. This company made what last year?"

He looks up and glares at the paper. "Eighteen million."

"That was the net. You need to look at all of your expenses."

Ryan looks at the papers in front of him again and starts crunching numbers. After a few minutes, he looks back up at me. "Gross would be eleven million nine hundred fifteen thousand one hundred ninety-seven."

"Good."

"Don't we have accountants for this shit?"

"We have several. But you need to know what you're doing so you can recognize if your accountant is fucking you over."

"Okay. I get it. I get why this is so important."

"Then get through the rest, and I'll show you how to input it since that's where you have issues."

He shakes his head and chuckles. "Can you believe we're all graduated from college and running our own companies?"

"Well, I'm running my own company, despite how small it is. You're running several."

"I can't believe Nick became a cop. Doesn't strike me as the type."

"Talking about me?" Nick says as he waltzes into the office dressed in his crisp New York Police Department uniform.

I grin. "We were reminiscing."

"Bullshit. We were trying to figure out how an asshole like you became a cop."

"Oh, that's easy. Watching your father get shot right in front of you and being pretty fucking convinced you're going to die in a hail of gunfire is a pretty damn good reason."

Ryan and I both smile a little weakly as Nick sits in an armchair. Since the night we rescued Mia and our father was shot, a lot of things have changed for us. All of us.

First and foremost, Ryan took control of the Crane Mafia immediately. He didn't have a choice. We never dreamed he'd have to take over this early. He hadn't gotten a chance to really do anything he wanted to in life. He was forced to get his business degree and couldn't finish school for culinary arts like he wanted to. Being able to explore that side of himself had been good for him, though. He needed to know that he's more than the mafia, and the mafia is more than him.

He'll never admit it, but he's needed these last few years to find himself and become the man that he is today. He's needed to see a world outside these walls so he knows what it is he's fighting for as he turns this mafia into what he wants it to be. How he envisions it.

Ryan looks at his watch and jumps up. "Fuck! I'm late. I need to get to L.A."

Nick and I both raise an eyebrow. I look at Ryan confused. "Why?"

"I… need to help a friend." He puts all of the papers away and strides out of the office, looking back over his shoulder at us when he reaches the door. "Lock up behind you when you leave. I'll be gone for a couple days."

"Yes, sir," Nick says, sticking out his tongue. Ryan laughs and leaves the room. Nick laughs.

"How was your first day?" I ask him.

"Not exactly my first day. First day on the streets with my FTO."

"What's an FTO?"

"Field Training Officer. He's kind of a dick. Doesn't believe I have any skills. He told me everything I learned in the academy was wrong, and I need to forget all of it."

I furrow my eyebrows. "That seems like the stupidest thing I've ever heard."

"He knows I'm part of the Crane family. He thinks because we have a new leader, he can push me around. I'm not worried about him."

"You think you'll like the job?"

He shrugs. "I don't know. All I know is I had to get out. That night, if I hadn't been keeping dad alive, I would've killed everyone. It would've been a bloodbath in there. And the scariest thing? I felt nothing. It's like all I could see was red. I was so pissed off that I fell off this cliff into this… I don't know… Darkness. It was terrifying and exhilarating at the same time. The fact that I was liking it, though. That's what scared me. That's what made me want to get out. I was on the path to becoming a fucking sociopath and not giving a single shit about it."

"I had never been so scared in my life. I saw dad laying on the ground. The gunfire didn't scare me. The blood. The guys on the ground…" I shake my head as I trail off. "None of that scared me. What scared me is the most invincible man I've ever met was bleeding out on the ground. My worst fear had come true. Someone close to me being hurt." I look down at my hands. "I wanted to tear them all apart. If Ryan hadn't

82

kicked us out, I would have. I would've crossed into that darkness you talked about without a second thought."

"That's why you started your business. Right out of college just like you wanted."

I laugh. "I'm still not out from under the mafia's thumb. All of my business is dad's contacts. All smaller mafias. I still have dirty money keeping my company afloat."

"You've only been up a few months. You'll get the business. Give it time. You have one or two other clients, don't you?"

I shrug. "A couple."

"You're taking off, Jas. Dad's doing well. He's almost completely recovered. Mom's coming back to herself after nearly losing her husband, and her kids. Ryan worked some voodoo with Lucinio Mafia so they aren't coming after us."

"Still don't know what that deal was."

"As long as it keeps us safe, I'm happy with it."

"I'm glad Mia's doing well. I don't blame her for moving to France. At least she gets to study under the best chefs in the world. I can't quite believe Ryan and the Commissioner have become so damn close." I laugh.

"Ryan is going to take this mafia to places we've never seen before."

I smile as I stand. Nick follows, and we walk out of the office. I look around the house as Nick and I leave. We lock up everything behind us and get in our cars, heading to a property I really want to buy. I pull out of the driveway, and Nick follows. I put the top down on my Corvette and crank up the stereo.

Ryan isn't only going to take this mafia far. He's going to take this family to places none of us have ever dreamed. He's going to build a legacy for himself that no one will ever meet or surpass. I can't wait to go along for the ride.

And what a hell of a ride it's going to be.

Chapter Twelve

✗ Nick ✗

"Just because you have a B.S. degree in Criminal Justice don't mean you know shit, rookie," my FTO says to me.

I turn my head and roll my eyes as I look out the window. Apparently, I don't know how to do traffic stops today. Truthfully, I've done everything correctly. I could name twelve things he's done incorrectly that could have gotten him killed. But sure. I'm the one who knows nothing. Doesn't take a genius to understand that leaning down and putting your face in front of someone else's is a good way to get your brains blown all over the street.

My phone vibrates in the breast pocket of my uniform. As the FTO, who I refuse to learn the name of, drives, I take it out and check my messages.

Commissioner Tate: How's the second day going? Better than yesterday?

I chuckle and shake my head. I take a quick glance at the FTO before typing out my reply.

Nick: Fucker is going to get himself and me killed. I swear to fuck. Walked up on a traffic stop. He walked around me. No

blocking. **Just leaned his fat ass down so he was eye level with the driver and starts talking to him. You know something is fucked up about that when the fucking gangster driver looks at the rookie cop confused as all fuck.**

Commissioner Tate: Christ. I'm hauling him in for retraining.

Nick: Then he tells me I'm the one doing something wrong. I'm not going to say I know everything there is to know out here, but I don't think it's a good thing when the rookie cop can train the senior officer better than what he's being trained.

Commissioner Tate: I'll have someone else out there with you tomorrow. In the meantime, make today work. Try not to get killed. Maybe attempt to save his life, too.

I grin a little wickedly and chuckle again.

"The girlfriend can wait," FTO Fuckface growls. "We're working."

The grin grows a lot more dangerous. "Not talking to my girl. Talking to your boss."

"The fuck?" He snaps his head towards me as he stops at a light.

I just shrug with the same grin and go back to my texts. It's probably a good way to make a few enemies, but I really don't give a shit. I don't think this fucker has many friends, and if he does, well, they probably all need a little extra attention from the Commissioner, too.

Nick: No promises.

Commissioner Tate: Ha! You're as much of an asshole as your brother.

Nick: Yeah, fucker taught us all well.

I put my phone away and completely ignore the glare FTO Little Dick is shooting at me as the light turns green. I look at the laptop screen in the squad and go through the calls. All cops have them in the squads. The calls that come in are sent to cops within the precincts the calls originate from. High priority calls are given to us via the radio and sent to our squad's laptop. The others are sent directly to the laptops in order to keep the radio as clear as possible for the high priority calls.

"There's a disturbance on Hook Creek," I say. "We can take that." I start to call in that we'll take the call, but I should really know better.

"You're not running the show, Crane. I am. We're not taking calls like that. You're not ready. We'll take the neighbor dispute."

I raise an eyebrow. "You're not serious. You're going to take a lower level call when this dispute has been on here for an hour."

"Disputes can turn ugly, rookie. You're not ready for it."

"I'm not ready for it? Or you're too lazy to take the calls you should? Our precinct is getting slammed here. You can't expect the cops we have on to clear all of these. Especially being short staffed."

"Take the neighbor dispute."

I sigh and rub my temple before taking the call and assigning it to us. I glance through the rest of the calls and already know which ones we'll be taking through the day. All of the easy ones. Noise complaint. Car break-in because it's already been done. We're just gathering evidence and doing a report. The domestics will be ignored unless he's forced to go. Considering he's avoided them thus far, I doubt we'll get them at all today.

✕ ✕ ✕

Hours later, when the shift from Hell is over, I sit in front of my locker, glaring. I've taken off my gear and shoved it all into my bag. Probably not the best idea, but I'm not sure I really give a shit. I can't take two more days of this shit until I get to my days off.

I rub a hand down my face when my phone starts ringing and sigh. I pick it up without looking at the caller ID because I'm really not in the mood to talk to anyone. "Yeah."

"Nick, what's wrong?" Jason asks.

I chuckle and shake my head. "Day two, and I'm already starting to miss the old days."

"Wow." Jason laughs. "Well, I was gonna ask if you wanted to help me move some shit to my new house."

"Oh fuck. You closed already?"

"Paid in cash. They seem to like that shit."

I laugh despite my piss poor mood. "I'll never get sick of making large purchases in cash." I glance up when I hear some voices and laughter. I sigh again. "Yeah, I can help move some shit. Might help work off some aggression."

"Nah. I have a better idea. Meet me at the club."

I smile. Jason has always known me well. "I'll meet you at home. I need to change and lock up my gear. God forbid I leave it in my trunk."

Jason laughs. "You'd get fired."

I grin. Leaving gear unattended is against department protocol. Someone in training asked about leaving it locked in their trunk if they decided to go out after their shift. Fucker was stupid enough to answer the trainer's questions about where and what kind of car he drives. He walked out from the club later that night with his trunk jimmied open, his car alarm going off, his gear missing, and a note pinned to his trunk floor where his gear had been saying he was fired.

As part of the mafia, I have a locked compartment in my trunk where I keep my gear. It's customized. We all have it. But I'm trying to be a good boy and leave all of that behind me. Following department rules is part of that.

After agreeing to meet me at home, Jason hangs up and I grab my gear. Hopefully, he's right. Maybe I need a few beers and a quick fuck. Tomorrow's a new day, right?

✗✗✗

"I mean, yeah, Jas, I guess, but that's a fucking huge undertaking," I say as I look down into the amber liquid in my glass.

"I know. But you did it with our house."

I sigh and look at my brother. "I know, but finding shit for our house is… fucking different. You want me to do it for your entire building and your house?"

The fucking asshole shrugs. "Not just that. Ryan's buildings, too."

"Jas, that's going to take a lot. Time. Effort. Research. Money."

"I know."

I watch him for a few moments before shaking my head and focusing back on the glass. "I can't do that. I don't have the time."

"I didn't want to pull this card, but you want us all to be safe, don't you?"

He knows he has me. I can hear it his fucking voice. I look back at him. "Anyone ever tell you you're a prick?"

He grins and takes a swig of his drink. "A lot."

I smile and chuckle. "It's gonna take time."

"I know. But you're the best. I don't trust anyone else. You know Ryan doesn't either. We need someone we know won't fuck us over because of who we are. You know your way around security. And you're really fucking good."

I finish off my beer and signal for another. "I can do it. And you know I will. But this shit takes time. I have to get the right stuff. You need to get me a layout of the buildings. I need to place orders. Things need to get upgraded and installed. This doesn't happen overnight. Especially with me actually working a real job now. My days aren't all that free. I can do what I can at night and on my days off."

Jason pats my back as the bartender puts another beer down in front of us. "Thank you. I appreciate it. You know I do. I'll feel better about all of this knowing you have my back."

"I'll always have your back, Jas." I take a drink before putting my glass down. "So, have you heard from Kelly?"

"Uh, yeah. Actually, she's one of my first clients. She has a building she bought in Austin, Texas for her design business. She'd like it remodeled. I'm heading down there this weekend."

"How's her boyfriend going to take her ex-boyfriend being the one to deal with the remodel?"

Jason laughs. "I was never her boyfriend. We fucked around. Haven't done anything since she met him and fell head over heels for him. That was like a year ago."

"At least she's happy."

"Thriving, too. Her designs are really taking off. It's incredible to see."

We both fall silent for a little while before I finally look at him again. "So, why did you bring me here? Just to beg me to help?" I grin at him.

He laughs. "No. Because I'm pretty sure you need to loosen up. We both do. Fuck, we've been on edge."

"The pick of women in this club doesn't look too promising tonight." I look over my shoulder and scan the crowd.

"Well, then standards will have to be lowered. Everyone wants a piece of the Crane brothers."

I laugh. "Lowering standards. You?"

He grins. "I'm fucking kidding." He points to a table at the other end of the club. "There's a girl's night going on. Two girls at that table are fucking hot. The other's are hot, but one is wearing a ring, and the other is very uninterested in her surroundings."

I grin as I follow his gaze. "That blonde is pretty damn gorgeous."

"The brunette sitting next to her is all mine. I had drinks sent over a little bit ago. I think it's time to introduce ourselves."

I follow my brother after calling for another round for their table. They're looking empty. I suddenly have high hopes this night won't suck as much as I thought it would.

XXX

The blond I set my sights on a couple hours ago is driving me completely insane. So crazy that I dragged her to the private bathroom in the VIP section and currently have her pressed against the wall with my tongue down her throat and fingers buried in her tight, wet heat.

I thrust my fingers in and out of her as I kiss her. "Fuck…," I groan when her hand finds my dick. She fumbles with my zipper but finally gets it down. I groan again when the skin of her hand meets my cock. She starts stroking.

"You're bigger than I thought," she whispers against my lips.

I thrust my fingers hard, deep, and fast. I rub her clit as I press down on it with my thumb. "Be sure to tell your friends." It's a cocky as hell statement, but I really don't give a shit.

She giggles. It's not sexy in the least, but my dick twitches anyway. She takes it as a sign that she's doing something right and strokes faster. I nip her neck when her pussy clenches tight around me, and she moans.

"Oh God, Nick."

"You should probably come." I twist my fingers inside her and thrust as I crook them against that sweet spot all women have but so few men know how to find. I take pride in the fact that, even though I'm drunk, I know exactly where it is. I keep rubbing my thumb against her clit and crooking my fingers inside her.

She digs her nails into my arm and shoulder and throws her head back. "Fuck!" Her hips jerk. Her pussy pulses uncontrollably as she comes. "Oh, Nick!"

I let her scream as loudly as she wants as she comes. I'm kind of a dick like that. I'll take her to a private area, but if anyone hears her outside these walls, that's something she'll have to deal with. I know perfectly well I'll end up in the tabloids. Girls like her always sell their story to them. But my brothers and I have become immune to all the bullshit.

I pull my fingers out of her. Normally, I'd lick her taste off them, but I've become admittedly jaded. Ever since what Penelope did to me, I've sworn off relationships and love. Fuck it all. Ryan and Jason were right. Love is a fucked up mess. I'd rather steer clear of it then go through the heartbreak again. We still don't know where the fuck she disappeared to.

I take a step back as the conquest of the night catches her breath. I pull a condom out of my wallet and put the wallet in my front pocket. Another thing I've learned from my brothers. Always wrap it up. Always know where the wallet is. Keep the condom with you until she's gone. Don't let her trap you. It took me a long time to listen, but fuck if I'm not now.

I unbuckle my belt and unbutton my jeans, then slide my zipper down. I pull myself out of my underwear and sheath my cock. The truth is, it took me a long time to truly view myself as an equal to them. Not because they ever made me feel differently. It was on me. I wasn't born into their family. It was something I always used as a type of division. A way to keep myself from forgetting where I came from.

Those walls came down the day Penelope walked. Now, I get it. I know that I'm equal to them. The world believes it. They believe it. Our whole family and mafia believe it. Me not believing it was doing nothing more than harming me. I'm a Crane. Just as Jason and Ryan are.

As soon as I'm covered, I pull the girl towards me. I grip her ass and lift her. I hold her between me and the wall. She wraps her arms around my neck and legs around my waist trembling and shivering in anticipation.

"I don't do relationships," I rumble against her lips. My dick twitches against her entrance as I push her panties aside once more. She's dripping for me.

90

"I know," she whispers. She wiggles, trying to get me to slide in. I hold her tighter against the wall, stilling her. This is my game. Not hers. I get the control.

"This happens one time. I don't ever give you seconds."

She giggles and tightens her grip on me. "The tabloids have you down pretty well."

I don't know why, but just that one statement angers the fuck out of me. I slam my dick into her and thrust hard. "You believe everything the tabloids say about me?"

She screams. "Oh fuck! Nick!"

I don't give her time to adjust to my size. I know I'm substantially larger than most. I'd usually be a nice guy and allow my partner to stretch around me. Why I don't let her is something I'm not really sure about. Maybe it's because she doesn't feel as tight around my cock as she did my fingers.

Or maybe it's because she doesn't seem to mind the hard and rough sex.

Keeping her pinned between the wall and me, I slam into her with each thrust. She claws at my back, giving me nothing but pants and moans as she meets me thrust for thrust. I feel her tightening around me and know she's close, but I'm not there yet. I'm not giving her what she wants until I get what I'm after.

My release.

I adjust my grip and slide my hands down to her thighs. I don't want her to move. I just want to pound my cock into her pussy until I'm ready to come. Whether she gets off isn't my concern. I tighten my grip. She bites my shoulder and hangs on tighter.

My thrusts become more erratic as I bury myself balls deep in her pussy each time I push my cock into her. The only thing I can hear now is the roar in my ears. All I can feel is the jolt of pleasure shooting down my spine and through my dick. I let my head fall back as I come, filling my condom with seed she'll never hope to have inside her. It'll be a cold day in hell before I give anyone that part of me. The only person who ever got close tried to destroy me, so fuck it all.

My hips jerk against hers as I blow my load. "Fuck, yes…," I moan. "Oh fuck."

"Nick, don't stop. Please, please don't stop," she pleads as she tries to wiggle herself against me.

I pull out of her as I catch my breath and lower her to the ground. "I'm done."

"W-what?"

I pull the condom off as I grab a paper towel. "I said I'm done." I don't look at her, but I can see her in the mirror above the bathroom counter biting her lip. I check my pocket for my wallet, smiling internally that it's still there. I don't know why, but it's always a relief when I feel it after sex with anyone.

"But the tabloids said -"

"That my latest fling said I'm the best fuck of her life? That I made her come like no other?" I turn a vicious glare on her while I wrap my condom in the paper towel. She has the decency to shrink away a little and look down. "Well, guess what, sweetheart? Maybe you shouldn't have brought up the tabloids. Maybe you shouldn't believe everything you read or hear about me." I shove the paper towel in my pocket and pack myself away. "Maybe we both would've enjoyed that a little more. Now, get out. I said I'm done."

She says nothing more, probably wise of her, and scurries out the door. I growl as I shake my head. I turn to the sink and splash water on my face after washing her scent off my fingers. When I'm finished and feel less like tearing apart the damn world, I make my own exit, running directly into Jason.

"The fuck was that about?" he asks with a slight grin.

I shrug and look down the hall after the girl. Her friends are hugging her and glaring at us. I look back at Jason. "She brought up the tabloids."

Jason throws his head back and laughs. "The familiar 'the tabloids said you're a great fuck' line?"

I grin as I follow him down the hall. We pass the girls' table. Neither of us so much as glance at them. "At least I got what I wanted."

Jason leads the way to his car. After we're both inside and he's driving towards home, he glances at me. "Feeling better?"

I smile and nod. "Yeah. Yeah, I needed that."

"I thought you might."

As Jason drives, I smile a little more. We've come far over the last couple of years. All of us. Ryan is settling into his role as Crane Mafia's fearless leader. Jason is going to take his company far. I know it.

And me? Well, I have plans to change the world right alongside my brothers. Whether that be as one of New York's finest, or the CEO of my own security firm, I don't know. Jason planted that thought today. I'm good at protecting my family. Maybe I can put those skills to good use someday and keep the innocent people of the world just as safe as I keep us.

Chapter Thirteen

☒ Ryan ☒

"I'm here," I say into my phone as I pace in front of the large floor to ceiling window in my penthouse. It overlooks downtown L.A.

"Ryan, this is bad. I don't know how to stop this," Alex Lucinio, my eighteen-year-old ally, says to me, his voice quivering.

He's next in line for Lucinio Mafia's throne. They're my biggest fucking rival. I should not have the type of relationship I have with Alex, but I do. I'm glad I spared him when we battled his father. He's a good kid. So is his brother. It isn't their fault their father is a damn psychopath with a death wish.

"We'll take care of it, Alex. Trust me," I say as soothingly as I can. I'm hoping the anger in my voice isn't evident. He doesn't need that.

"Ryan, I don't think you understand the plan tonight. He's going to decimate them. And he's making me lead. If I don't do this, he'll probably fucking kill me."

Alex is panicking because the gang he's about to go after is my ally. And since he's my ally, it means he's going after his own ally. I can see how he'd be freaking out. Fuck. I would be, too.

But I'm not because I have a plan. A plan I haven't had a chance to tell him because I haven't had the time. He keeps getting interrupted when we talk, and I'm starting to think his fucking phone is tapped. Probably paranoia because the kid is really good. He knows how to check for that shit.

"Meet me at my penthouse. We're not discussing this now. I have a plan. A plan that I assure you will work. We just need to play our cards correctly."

"How are you so calm and collected?"

I chuckle. "It's a gift. One you'll learn as the years go by. Now, calm down. Are you bringing your brother?"

He sighs with a low growl. "No. I'm sorry, man. He, uh…" Alex pauses, and I furrow my brows. "He…" He sighs. "Fuck. Dad got him. He said he wanted to lead this one. He was beaten down. He has a broken arm this time."

"Christ." I let out my own growl. Far more dangerous. "Motherfucker is gonna get what's coming to him one day."

"Just… let me take over first. I need to make sure everything is in place for Josh."

"I know, Alex. I made a promise. I won't go after him unless I absolutely need to, and I'll make sure you know, so we can combine forces."

I can hear Alex flying through the streets as he drives towards my penthouse. I walk to my couch and sit down, propping my feet up on the coffee table in front of me. I turn when Charlie gets off the elevator. It opens right in my foyer. I haven't decided how I feel about that feature, but given I own the building and had the security upgraded, it freaks me out a little less. No one has access to this floor unless I want them to.

"I'm almost there."

"You have access. Just come up. Charlie just got here. We'll talk about it before we go out there."

"I really hope your plan is gold, Ryan."

I chuckle. "Trust me." I hang up as Charlie sits down in a chair next to the couch.

He waits for me to hang up before he speaks. "You need a second in command."

I blink. "I have one." I gesture to him.

95

"Until I retire. Soon."

"Fuck, don't you dare. Not yet. Just give me time to fucking get my bearings here." I shoot him a glare. "I need you."

He laughs. "I didn't fucking say tomorrow, Ryan. But I am getting up there in age. I'm not as quick on my feet as I used to be. We talked about this. You have a year to figure it out. I'm not gonna leave you high and dry. You're like a son to me. But I do want to enjoy my wife and family before I kick the bucket. Maybe travel and see the world. You know, with them." He grins. "Not you."

I laugh. "Fine, fine. I'll start the process. But not tonight. What do you got for me? Are we set up?"

He nods and leans forward. "Yep. I talked to the leader of the Sabers. They know the plan. But you need to make sure Alex knows his role."

"He'll do what needs to be done. It's the only way we can protect him and the Sabers."

"You know how unorthodox this is. Your father would go after the Lucinio's."

I bristle a little but keep my cool. I level Charlie with a glare that has him backing down instantly. "I'm not my father."

He holds his hands out as he leans back in his chair. "You're not, Ryan. I'll be the first to admit you're a lot darker. Fucking ruthless. But your methods are different. It's just taking some getting used to."

"Charlie, you know I respect the hell out of you. But you and everyone else need to fall in line with the changes. I might still be finding my footing, but I know where I want to take us. I've been leading battles for a long fucking time. I'm not letting one of the good guys down over some fucked up thinking of his father."

Before Charlie has a chance to say anything more, the elevator dings. Alex steps off, chewing his lip and dressed in his gear. His bulletproof vest is snuggly in place. He has a gun on his hip and one strapped to his leg. If I didn't trust him, I'd be a little worried at how he could easily take me out right now.

Charlie, my ever loyal second in command, is a lot less trusting of Alex than I am. He almost jumps out of his skin when he sees him, and looks at me with horror. I don't miss the hand on the butt of his gun at his hip.

Alex shoots him a glare. "Oh, calm the fuck down. If I wanted to kill you or him, I would've stepped off the damn elevator shooting."

I can't help but chuckle. "Kid has a point."

Alex jabs a finger in my direction and levels the dark glare on me. "Don't call me kid. I'm fucking six years younger than you are, you asshole."

I bite my lip to keep from laughing. Charlie, on the other hand, howls with it as Alex sits down. Fucker holds his sides and throws his head back, laughing manically. I grin and shake my head. Alex is one of the only people in the world who has ever talked to me in that manner. And I allow it because I've started to think of him as family. He's proven himself on the right side, my side, more times than I can count over the past two years.

Probably one of the only reasons I let him get away with talking to me like that. Fuck knows no one but my family is allowed to. And even then I sometimes put them in their place.

"So, what are we doing, Ry? Because I'm fucking freaking out a little bit with this one. I have guys waiting on orders. Where I want them to show up. I'm stalling, and my dad is getting pissed." Alex's piercing blue eyes burn into me. He's trying to be hard, but I can see the fear.

"First of all, you need to trust in me and your allies. I'm here to help you. We all are. Second, you have to learn to trust yourself. You've been running missions for a long time. You, Gavin, Damon, and Josh. You have people within those walls who will follow you over your father. Use them. You're not going to make it in this world if you don't trust in your skills and abilities out there. Your instincts. If something seems off to you, it probably is."

"I know, Ryan." He scrubs his hands down his tired face. "Fuck, I know." He leans forward. "It's not that I'm not confident. I am. I do trust you. But he's picked the team. I don't have Gavin, Damon, or Josh tonight. It's just me out there."

I shake my head. "No. It's not just you. You have people on your side, Alex. You have me, my team, and the Sabers. We're your allies."

He nods and takes a shaky breath. "What's the plan?"

"Call your team to the Sabers' hideout. I'll tell you on the way." I stand and follow behind Alex and Charlie to the elevator.

In a few hours, this entire mess will be put behind him.

Us.

By the time I'm done with Alex Lucinio, he'll be one of the best trained mafia leaders the world has known. Even if he has no desire to take on the role. Through him, Josh Lucinio will become a formidable leader in his own right. I might only know him through reputation, and from what I've learned from Alex, but I trust that he'll take the Lucinio Mafia in the right direction.

✘✘✘

"Ready?" I ask Alex when we show up at the Sabers' hideout.

I look over at him from the driver's seat of my black Ford Escape with tinted windows. The tint is illegal, but it helps being who I am. If I get stopped for it, which is rarely, I never get ticketed. As soon as they see my driver's license, they're done with me.

He sighs. "Yeah, I guess. I'm not looking forward to walking my ass into a building rigged to fucking explode."

I chuckle. "I don't blame you." I reach between us and hold up a small black cylinder with a red button on top as I smile. "But it's not going to do shit until the button is pushed. I'm the only one who has the control. You know the code word. Use it when you're out of harm's way. The house won't explode until then. I'll have eyes on you the whole time. Not just my guys, but me."

"And Charlie has my car?"

"Yep." I flick my head behind us. "He's pulling up now."

"And you're sure this is going to work? They're not going to turn on us?"

I raise an eyebrow. "Okay, I need to ask. What the fuck is wrong with you? You've grown pretty damn confident over the past couple of years. You always have been, but today... something is off."

Alex closes his eyes and lets out a long breath as his head falls back against the headrest. "Something big is going on, Ry. I can't figure it out. He's so fucking secretive. And vicious." He shakes his head and opens his eyes as he looks at me. "Something is really fucking off with him. He's even jetting off all the damn time and being dodgy as hell about why. And then the thing with Josh? I don't even know how the hell it happened. It was so fucking fast. And he waited until I was fucking away from it. I didn't know shit about it until I went to Josh's room to see if he was ready to go. He was fucking groggy as hell and passed out mid-conversation. Just said he felt out of it. Exhausted as fuck."

I shake my head. "Alex, I promise you, bro. Your father will get what's coming to him. Keep an eye on him. Tell me what's going on. I'll be here for you. You know that."

"I know, Ry. You don't know how much I appreciate you."

I reach over and squeeze his shoulder. "I know. And I appreciate you and the help you're always willing to give. Now what do you say we get you out there? We need to end this bullshit."

Alex nods and steps out of the car. He walks to his. Seconds later, I can hear some shuffling. "You got me?" he asks over our earpieces.

"I got you," I say.

"Son of a bitch. I'm fucking nervous."

I watch as he pulls away from our gathering point. "Don't be. You got this. You're a good leader. You've got eyes all over the place on you. And nothing is going to happen until you give me the code word."

A few minutes later, he sighs as he pulls into the meeting place with his team. "I'm here," he murmurs. I hear his door close after he steps out. He clears his throat. "Alright, listen up," he commands. I grin because his voice has taken on that confidence he's gathered over the past couple of years is very evident. "Everyone have earpieces?"

"Got them," several voices murmur.

"Geared up?

"Yes, sir," more voices say.

"Let's get this over with. I'm fucking tired of being run ragged," Alex growls.

I can't help but grin wider. "Sassy motherfucker," I say.

Alex doesn't respond to me, but I know him well enough to know he's grinning cockily to himself. I watch from my vantage point as he leads his team down a small hill to a house below where I'm sitting. No one would know I'm here, but I can see everything I need to. Including the back door they're about to bust down.

I watch as half of his team walks to the front door. When they're all in position, Alex takes a breath. I can't hear what they're saying to him over their earpieces, but I can hear everything he says and everything the people around him do.

"On my count," Alex says quietly. "Three... Two... One... Enter!"

I watch as both teams, Alex leading the team at the back door, kick the doors open simultaneously. It's truly impressive to watch a young man leading a team with such precision. I can't help but see myself in him because he really is good at what he does. He has a big heart, and he's truly fucking confident.

"Give them time to search a little bit before you find the note. It's on the door leading to the basement. First door you come to when you leave the kitchen."

After a few moments, Alex inhales sharply. "What the fuck?" There's a quiver in his voice. For a second, I'm fucking terrified something has gone wrong. I start quickly getting out of my SUV. "You fuckers think I didn't know you're coming? Fuck you. Enjoy the show. Tic-toc, assholes." He pauses after reading the note out loud. My heart rate returns to normal. Add phenomenal fucking actor to his list of attributes. "Christ. Everyone out! Out! Out!"

I grin as I watch everyone scatter. I'd laugh, but I want Alex to focus. He should be in the goddamn theater. Not leading a fucking mission. His performance convinced me, and I'm the one who set the whole thing up.

Alex commands his team back up the hill. I'm completely amazed at how well everyone is listening to him. He has never had the amount of control I've had over the teams he's led in the past. He has led, but he's always had his father looking over his shoulder.

"Baboon's ass," Alex growls.

I glance over the area, making sure everyone is clear of the scene. At least enough that no one will get hurt when I denote the explosives that will bring the dilapidated house to the ground. Alex's team is close, but not close enough to be hurt.

"All teams clear, sir," one of my own guys says to me.

"Bomb's away," I say with a far too evil grin and low chuckle.

I settle back as I press the button and watch the explosion. The house practically combusts. The houses on the entire block the house I blew up is on are empty. All except the one on the corner. We found a squatter there and removed him. The rest of the block could use some development. I figure I'm helping out the city by demolishing the eyesores.

Considering the amount of explosives used, I think we did a good job. As Alex and his team reach the top of the hill and jump in vehicles, I reach down and find another remote.

"Fuck, Ryan. Enough TNT?" Alex asks, out of breath. I can hear his tires squealing as he pulls away. "I expected a fireball at my back."

"Not done yet," I say.

"Fuck, you're fucking crazy, Crane." I hear him laugh. "Don't wreck my city, you motherfucker. I'm going home to sleep."

"Aww. Don't wanna watch the show?" I hit another button and watch each house on the block explode. "Why the hell hasn't the city done this already?" I ask.

Alex laughs. "Because they're too busy fighting crime and drugs to develop the hood. Besides, they make a lot of money keeping it like that. I heard it's in historical L.A. or some shit."

I crack up. "Well, guess they ain't getting any more from that."

When the last house falls to the ground after it explodes, I set my detonator down and survey my handiwork. Maybe Jason can work out a deal and put up housing or something for low-income families. He's not into real estate exactly, but I know he has friends who are.

"Ready to move out, Ry?" Charlie asks me as he slides into the passenger seat next to me.

I look over at him. "Ready to go home. I miss my damn bed. I need to stop staying up for hours on end putting together missions without sleep."

Charlie chuckles. "I'd agree with you, but I know you better than that. It's not the way you work. You fucking thrive on no sleep. I can't figure out how."

"It's a gift."

I grin as he laughs. I start driving towards the airport. Usually, I'd stay an extra day, but I don't want to this time. I miss my family, though I'd never tell them. I want to talk to Nick about building security. I know Jason talked to him. He agreed to help out, but I have a few requests I'm hoping he can deliver on. I trust he can because he's the best, whether he wants to admit it or not.

I drive in silence to the airport and board my jet without saying a word. I walk directly to my bedroom and yawn as I fall onto the bed. For the first time in a very long time, I actually feel confident in where we're all going.

Nick, while I don't think he's quite where he wants to be, is doing what he chooses for once. Not what he's told. It's the first time he's truly done that in the entire time I've known him. Even with Penelope, he did what he thought was the right thing. What society has conditioned us all to believe. Marry the person you've spent so many years with. Thankfully, we were able to protect him from the level of damage she could have leveled on him.

Jason, while he's not completely out from under the mafia's thumb, is thriving. I've never seen him so happy. To be running his own company and not running missions has gotten Jason out of his shell. He's always had the ruthlessness in him, but he's far better at letting it out in the boardroom as opposed to the streets. Not to say he can't be fucking vindictive when he wants to be. I've seen him take people out without batting an eye. Most of the time, he struggles with it. But when he knows the fuckers deserve every bullet they're introduced to, he doesn't feel an ounce of regret.

My father, even though he hates not being out here with me, is adjusting to his new life. A life away from the mafia. He's happily jetting my mother all over the world and lavishing her with all of the love she deserves.

We've all come so far. Nick, Jason, and I are all really just beginning our lives. I'm really fucking excited to see where we all end up.

The End

Next In The Crane Family Series

The dark and sexy Crane Family Series continues with **Sweet Lies**.

I never saw Jessa coming, but sitting next to her in class was the best decision I've ever made. Her wide, innocent eyes haunt my dreams, and I can't stop thinking about my lips on hers.

She's made for me.

Mine.

Then, my mafia boss father becomes obsessed with my sexy, beautiful girlfriend. Complications inevitably arise. He's not getting his hands on my girl.

Despite my billions and unlimited resources to keep her hidden from my family, my father sets his sights on my girl. I discover real quick just how far I'll go to be her fiercest defender.

But she begins acting strange. Fearful.

To protect her, I have two choices. Unleash a darkness that I've fought so hard to keep hidden deep within…

…or leave…

~ This book is a steamy College/Mafia Romance that has dark and violent themes, child abuse, mental health themes, emotional abuse, DA, physical assault, mental abuse, and strong language that may not be suitable for all readers. ~

Order *Sweet Lies* Today!

The Crane Family Series

Available Now

The Reluctant Mafia King
Sweet Lies
Billion Dollar Love Story
Be Mine
Protecting Her
Dangerously Forbidden Love
His Heart
Love In The Dark

Box Sets Available

The Crane Family Series

Other Books By Melony Ann
The Beautiful Dream Series

Available Now

Loving You
My Love, My Heart
Softening Lyric
Undercover Temptations
Captain Charming
Breaking Boundaries
Crashing Into You
Tactical Inferno
Ravishing Our Queen
Cherished By The Texan
Unveiling Our Passions

Box Sets Available

The Beautiful Dream Series: Box Set: Part 1
The Beautiful Dream Series: Box Set: Part 2

The Deimos Trilogy

Available Now

Connor's Legacy
Aryan's Alpha
Kade's Redemption

Box Sets Available

The Deimos Trilogy

The Forbidden Temptation Series

Available Now

The Detective's Forbidden Temptation
The Running Back's Forbidden Temptation

The Lucinio Family Series

Available Now

Rising From The Ashes
The Player's Rebel
Encrypting My Heart

Multi Author Series
Piper Falls: Firehouse 49

Available Now

Ignite My Fire by Melony Ann
Regain My Fire by Kindra White
Playing With My Fire by D.L. Howe
Fight My Fire by Darley Collins
Against My Fire by Anneke Boshoff
Relight My Fire by Louise Murchie
Harness My Fire by Ayana Lisbet
Quench My Fire by Havana Wilder

Let's Be Friends

Follow me on

Bookbub

Facebook

Goodreads

Instagram

Tik Tok

Visit my website
www.melonyannauthor.com

Subscribe to my newsletter and get a FREE never-seen-before NOVELLA
just for subscribers!
https://www.melonyannauthor.com/exclusive-content

Join my Facebook Reader Group!
Jason's and Melony's Sizzling Book Nook

The official Crane Family Series Playlist on YouTube
https://youtube.com/playlist?list=PLGEiD5wbQmDc78K7gNeODh-janqmIFiie

Dedication

Always guiding us forward, pushing us to do our best. Never leaving us behind or alone.

Acknowledgements

Brad - Thanks for loving me in ways I never dreamed possible. You are, and always will be, the love of my life. I truly love you.

Laura - The sunshine that brightens my day. My heart. I truly love you.

Jay - Thanks for being my best friend and so, so much more. My protector. My love. I love you so, so damn much.

Dan Rengering - Not only are you an awesome cover model, but you're an incredible person and an amazing defender of me and other authors in this community. Thanks for being a part of this and giving me the courage to publish. You know I never would have published my first book without you.

Ayana - Thank you so much for all you do for me and so many. Love you!

Anneke - Thank you for inspiring me each day with your kindness. Love you!

Jason - I would not be going wide with these books without you. Thank you for getting me through this.

To the Bookstagram Community.

To my family.

To all of those who believe in me and support me.

To all of those who don't.

Cover by: Carter Cover Designs

Cover Model - Dan Rengering

Photographer - Jean Woodfin of JW Photography

Edited by: Alyssa Skaggs

About Melony Ann

Melony Ann began writing short stories and poetry as a child. She continued honing her craft over the years until she took the plunge and began publishing her work, despite having severe anxiety.

Melony writes contemporary romance stories that are full of suspense and a lot of steam.

When she isn't writing, she is loving her family and working to make her life something she deserves.

Melony believes that if her writing can inspire just one person, then all of her hard work is worth it.

Her hope is that her writing allows each and every one of her readers to escape for a little while. To dive into a different world one book at a time.